DIAMOND

DIAMOND

by

Julia Erickson

Chinquapin Press

United States of Amcrica

ISBN:978-1-942006-13-8

Cover design by Julia Erickson

First Printing

To Victoria G.

Your friendship and encouragement have meant so much to me. Thank you for being my "biggest fan"!

PROLOGUE

Three Years Earlier

It was supposed to be a simple info pickup from an informant, but shortly after Bryce swaggered into the pizza parlor, thumbs in his pockets, he sensed something amiss. Dim wattage from the lamps over the scarred tables emitted only meager light. The oily smell of greasy pepperoni permeated the air.

But it was the shifty glances from the seedy diners and a crawly feeling on his skin of being under observation that triggered his unease.

He inquired at the cash register about the "special order" he was there for – one extra-large Meat Lover's pizza, with a packet of secrets sealed in plastic underneath.

The informant's eyes were open wide – too wide. "Afraid there's been a mistake." The thin black man trembled, a vein pulsing in his temple.

Bryce leaned back casually and took a leisurely glance around. That was when he spotted him.

Heavily tattooed ham-hock arms. Yellow eyes, glaring at him. Stringy moustache. Back in the kitchen, slumped against the wall, visible through the doorway – *Habrin Merkochaz.*

The man's ugly features were straight from the Agency training class, and burned into his memory. A lethal character, wanted for despicable things, including human trafficking and murder in the first degree.

His first mission as a rookie agent, and already he faced an impossible choice.

The still, small voice inside came as a clear beacon through his fog of uncertainty. "Go for it."

Okay, Lord, if you say so!

He hopped over the counter, one hand on it for stability, and drew both handgun and radio, raising one to his ear and the other in the direction of the criminal.

"Backup, I need backup now." His radio buzzed as he relayed the message. "Hands up. You're under arres-"

The whistle of a bullet nearly piercing his earlobe interrupted him. He whirled to see a beefy bodyguard stalking out from behind a refrigerator, aiming a pistol for his skull.

One shot from him clipped the man's shoulder, throwing the guy off balance, and his head cracked against the razor-sharp corner of an industrial oven. He slumped to the ground, unconscious.

Bryce whipped the gun back up and centered it on the obese form of Merkochaz. "Hands up."

"All riiight, ssso ya got meee." The man slurred, seeming more than a little intoxicated.

He lowered his gun a fraction. "Yes, so if you'll kindly turn and face the wa-"

Merkochaz chose that moment to lunge down and fling the oven door open, blasting a wave of heat into the air as he seized the pan of baking pizza with his huge bare hands and hurled it at Bryce.

"*Aaah!*" Bryce got splatted in the face with half-baked Hawaiian ham and pineapple - then the desperate criminal reached into the oven and scooped up two enormous handfuls of smoking ashes, pitching them in his direction.

Rookie mistake! He felt like an idiot. The man was obviously *not* drunk, if the speed with which he was heading for the door was any indication.

He fired. The bullet pierced the man's thick, blubbery thigh and he collapsed with a shriek of pain. The yellow eyes glared pure hatred at him, like a caged puma.

Boom! Just when he had the upper hand, Bryce was tackled from behind. He caught a glimpse of a man's uniformed shoulder as his cheek smashed into the gritty ash-covered floor. Somebody in the pizzeria must have called 911, slightly disturbed by the gunfire in the kitchen.

"Special Agent!" He grunted in frustration. "Back left jeans pocket."

"Oh." The policeman rolled off of him after finding the Agency ID. "Sorry. I just saw you shooting..."

"Yeah, well, that man is a hot number on our most wanted list. Slap a pair of metal bracelets on him, will ya?" Bryce brushed the charred coals and ash from his shirt front as he leaped to his feet. Only then did he realize his radio was crackling. "Agent Reynolds?! Come in, Agent Reynolds!" It was his boss.

He grabbed it. "Here."

"Bryce! What's going on? We're getting alerts-"

"Merkochaz." The one word from him stopped the irritated flow of his boss's speech.

"Did you just say *Merkochaz?!*"

"He's in custody, Sir. I had to shoot his bodyguard. I have a witness..." He looked at the black man, who stood horrified in the doorway, and read the name tag pinned to his t-shirt. "...a witness named Dave. And a policeman showed up, with, I assume, more on the way." He was pleased that his voice remained cool.

"Okay. Listen to me. Freeze it. Don't go anywhere, don't let Merkochaz or the witness out of your sight, lock down the pizza place! We'll be there in five."

"Got it."

Soon, the pizza parlor swarmed with agents. They'd hustled Merkochaz into a bulletproof ambulance and the body of the guard was taken away.

"Bryce, I'm surprised." Mr. Montrose's coffee-colored face was unreadable. Not even a twitch of his moustache betrayed his thoughts.

"Sir?"

"You did exactly the right thing. I'm shocked that you had the guts. Most newbies flinch in the face of a challenge like you had today."

Bryce blinked. His eyes still stung from the charred ash specks. "I felt that it was what I had to do, Sir."

"I have to say, I'm impressed. You 'burned through the ashes', so to speak, to see right to the heart of that scene." A smile creased Monty's face. "Which brings me to your new code name."

Code name? I've finally earned one!

"Ashburn." Monty nodded. "Yep. That's it. Ashburn."

Bryce rolled the name around in his mind. *Ashburn.* He laughed. "I like it!"

Monty grinned. "It's yours. I'll put it on file when I get back to the Agency." He slapped Bryce on the back and walked off, barking orders to the others.

Ashburn. It would be a reminder for the rest of his days of how he'd followed that inner voice. But he'd gotten ashes thrown in his face because he had been caught unawares. Embarrassing.

I will never get caught off guard again.

CHAPTER ONE

Wedding Bells are Ringing

Penny's eyes flew open. *Of all the days to forget to plug in my phone, I had to choose this one!* The dead little iPhone didn't even have one feeble spark of energy left, and consequently the alarm she'd set had *not* rung.

Penny dashed into her closet and jerked a favorite peacock-blue blouse from a velvet hanger, then snatched a pair of sandals and some dark jeans as if she were a starving beggar grabbing a loaf of bread.

"I'm gonna be late!" She hollered, knowing nobody but a cat and a canary could hear her. "I can't *believe* it!" She dragged a hairbrush through her wild mane of dark red hair and splashed her face with cold water. The mascara would have to be foregone. She'd stabbed herself in the eye once while applying it in the car and sworn "Never again".

Her kitten, Dot, came running at the sound of her mistress's cries of dismay. She mewed, cocking her head inquisitively.

"It's ok, Dot, mummy's just having a nervous breakdown." Penny cooed. "Couldn't you have woken me up with a soft little paw to the nose? Ohh, right, that's only for Saturday mornings when I *want* to sleep in..." She trailed off and gazed at the tiny cat.

"Oh, come here, you." She picked up the bundle of warm fuzz and held it under her chin. If there wasn't time to cuddle one's kitten, the world had come to an end.

Penny watched as Cara emerged from the dressing room in the beautiful bridal store and mounted a round platform in front of a three-way mirror.

She tingled from the waves of emotion sweeping over her. Joy for her dearest friend mingled with dark undertones of secret grief. Or maybe it was the unsatisfying egg McBiscuit she'd wolfed down on the way to the appointment. "Babydoll, you look like a princess."

Cara turned, layers of the creamy satin bridal gown swishing silkily as she spun before the triple-sided mirror. "What do you think?" Her hushed voice sounded delicate, in the way one would touch a rose petal, fearful of crushing it.

They'd been shopping in the swanky Atlanta store for hours as Cara tried on dresses. The difficulty of finding just the right dress had been compounded by the fact that her friend was on a quest to find a wedding gown that modestly covered both shoulders and bust. Cara would have no plunging neckline or strapless dress, which narrowed the options.

But now they'd found it. *The one.*

"It's so gorgeous, the beauty is hurting my eyes!" *There. Lifesaving, hurt-hiding humor. Never fails.*

Cara's laughter rippled from her like a brook tumbling down a mountainside. "I think this might be it." She turned back to the mirror and studied her reflection with a wondering look.

The light cap sleeves graced Cara's straight shoulders with a touch of lace. The dress sparkled with glittering glass crystals and embroidery, sloping down to hug Cara's slim waist and then flaring out in an impossibly full skirt falling all the way to the floor in a frothy waterfall of shimmering fabric layers.

Cara's eyes were alight like candle flames. "Penny, I think I've fallen in love with this dress."

"It looks like it loves you too." She grinned mischievously and they both giggled like schoolgirls.

Her tall, slim, pretty friend looked like a model. In fact, she'd been approached by a bridal dress TV show to participate in one of their episodes, but had politely declined.

Cara nodded a firm nod. "I'm going to bring back Mom and Nana to have a look at this one."

Penny waited while Cara slipped into the dressing room again to change out of the dream dress.

Oh Father. This is harder than I thought it would be. Please remove my selfish thoughts from my own past and help me as I rejoice with my dear friend over this blessed upcoming marriage.

But try as she might, her mind rebelled, running back to thoughts of the one she had loved and lost, gone now beyond her reach. The young man with those kind eyes, that gentle smile. Penny breathed a sigh.

God, you're going to have to help me through this wedding, because I can't handle it on my own.

Bryce sank his teeth into the juicy hamburger and looked around the patio where they had spent so many summer evenings, having cookouts with Gram and Gramps. Now, although his grandparents were gone, the family still gathered around the spacious outdoor table, enjoying the breeze and the bright yellow-orange of the budding sunset. Visits to his family home in Colorado were rare, so each one was treasured.

Cara's expression, already happy, blossomed into something deeper as their gazes met. Her beautiful gray eyes shimmered with a touch of soft blue, something they only did when she was feeling peaceful and content. He was still floored by the way they seemed to change shades to match her mood.

Conversation flowed easily around the table as one-by-one, everyone around the table won clean-plate-awards. For dessert, his mom pulled out a trifle layered with cool whip, Reese's peanut butter cups, and something smooth and chocolatey. Nutella, maybe.

About halfway through her serving of the trifle, the conversation turned to the upcoming wedding.

After his romantic scavenger-hunt style proposal, he and Cara had enjoyed an upscale dinner at the Alvaton banquet hall with all their family and closest friends, but they had not revealed location of the wedding, only the date, June 2nd.

So now, his mother, brother, and sister were on the edge of their seats.

"Okay. The secret's out. Turtle Bay Resort, in Oahu, Hawaii!"

A chorus of excited exclamations went up all around the table. Cara's face glowed.

"Ooooh!" Bethany's starry eyes widened. "And you're flying the guests in?"

"Yes." He answered for both of them. "About fifty of them."

They discussed details as they cleared up the table and washed up the dishes all together. The ceremony would be performed by his good friend and pastor, Matt Laramie. Cara had chosen the wedding colors... silver, and a soft shade of aquamarine. The flowers would be white gardenia blossoms, white roses, and white hibiscus flowers. She'd asked her best friend Penny to be Maid of Honor. Blake, of course, was his Best Man.

"And Bethany... I would be so happy if you would be my bridesmaid."

His shy little sister had warmed up to Cara, so much so that now she threw her arms around her in a big hug. "Of course!"

And then, to his surprise, Blake loudly cleared his throat. "Hey guys... I have some news."

The rest of the family looked at each other in surprise, and waited for Blake to continue.

"I'm moving. To Atlanta." In the stunned silence, he hesitantly continued. "You know how Mr. Kendall has wanted to retire for years... well, he's finally doing it."

For Cara's benefit, Blake explained that Mr. Kendall was his boss of three years, whom he worked for as a realtor. "He's closing down his whole real estate agency, and I'm transferring to a different office."

"Blake, this is... astounding." Bryce found his voice from wherever it had fled. "I thought you were going to stay here with the ladies." He eyed his mom and Bethany, and sent a piercing look towards his younger brother.

"I thought so too... but life happens, you know? And the suburbs of Atlanta are a booming realty area." Blake sighed, and then brought his gaze up to meet Bryce's once more. "I think I could do well there."

His mother gently laid a hand on Bryce's arm. In her wise face, he could read everything she would have said. Blake was right. He would do very well in Atlanta as a realtor... he had the guts, hutzpah, and sheer outgoing, upbeat personality to succeed in a fiercely competitive field.

But oh, they would miss him.

"Maybe we'll move back to Georgia with you, Blake." Dawn Reynolds shrugged her shoulders and smiled. "It will be so very quiet around this house without you two boys."

Bethany expressed her affirmation of her brother's decision, and then they all discussed the job change at length – Blake filled in some of the details and told them a little more about what he had been planning and dreaming.

After dropping his bomb, Blake asked him if he'd come see his latest LEGO creation. "I know it's hard to tear yourself from her side," He smiled at Cara, "But it's cool, I built a replica of Castle Entführt to scale. It's an old stone fortress in Germany."

Cara's face tightened at the mention of that particular castle, which just so happened to be the one they'd seen only a few weeks ago, when they'd rescued a kidnapped technology developer and uncovered proof of an illegal arms dealership.

He cleared his throat as they left the table. "So, uh, how did you decide to copy that particular castle?"

"Oh, I found it on Google Earth. It looked pretty neat."

You should see the real thing sometime. "I see." He followed his brother up the stairs to the room they had shared as boys, before he went off to college.

His attention was instantly captured by the towering mini-structure on the table by the window. Blake had done a remarkable job replicating the castle with LEGO bricks. Bryce could even see the spot on the river where the notorious Ryan Black had fallen to his death from the high stone wall.

"Nice job."

"Hey, Bryce?"

At the lost-little-boy tone in his brother's deep voice, he looked up from studying the castle's intricacies.

For once, Blake's face was sober, his mouth set in a grim line. "What about... Dad?"

The sudden anger roiling in his gut was an ugly shock. "What do you mean?" His own voice had morphed into a growl.

"Are..." Blake hesitated, cocking his head, "Are you going to tell him you're getting married?"

"*No!*" The word ripped from his throat and struck the air full-blast. The echo rang in his ears like the aftermath of a dynamite explosion. He looked at the hurt spreading across Blake's face and cringed. "Blake, I'm sorry. I'm not mad at *you*."

Blake's expression cleared. "It's ok. I know."

Their eyes locked in a look of mutual understanding. They'd bonded together even tighter after their father deserted them when he was fourteen and Blake just-turned-twelve. But he was the one who'd had to rise up and become the man of the house. He didn't think Blake ever felt the same level of pressure as he did. He'd been the responsible protector, Blake the happy-go-lucky sidekick.

He picked up a stray LEGO plant piece and snapped it on the corner of the castle landscape. "Even if I wanted to, I don't know where to reach him."

"Couldn't you…" Blake looked unsure of what his reaction might be, but pressed ahead, "you know, with your government connections, whatever they are… couldn't you look for him?"

The Agency could probably track down Greg Reynolds in a heartbeat. Or at the most, three days. Not that he'd tried. He wasn't ready to face the turmoil that would cause. He'd rooted out the black, rotten growth of bitterness from his heart, but it was still raw and painful. The healing balm of forgiveness wasn't yet finished with its work.

"I'm afraid that's not possible." The white lie stung for a moment, but he shrugged it off.

TWO MONTHS LATER

A knock sounded on the front door as they were assembling wedding invitations. Her mother and grandmother looked up, surprised expressions on their sweet faces.

Cara popped up from her seat. "I'll get it."

She walked through the door of the dining room where they were working and out down the hallway to the front door of her grandmother's aged-but-attractive house and swung it open.

"Oh my-" Before she could get anything else out, her face was pressed against the chest of the man gathering her close in his arms.

Bryce kissed the top of her hair. "Hey."

She tilted her face up. *"Bryce!"* *Oh Lord, how I love this man.*

He grinned down into her eyes. "I know. I love you too."

"Cara? Is that Bryce?" her mother's voice drifted down the hall.

She pitched her voice at a whisper as she drank in the sight of his smile. "I thought I wouldn't get to see you again until the ceremony!"

Bryce tugged her closer. "Here I am."

Then she called out from inside the safe circle of her fiancé's embrace. "Yes, Mom, Bryce is here! What a surprise!" They slowly let go of each other and moved to the dining room for Bryce to greet the ladies.

"It's wonderful to see you again, young man." Nana beamed at Bryce with genuine delight on her faintly wrinkled face.

Bryce bowed in her direction. "It's my pleasure."

Mom got up to give Bryce a hug. "Welcome back to Georgia! How is it that this surprise came to be?"

"Well..." He nudged Cara's elbow. "I was suffering from withdrawal."

Feminine laughter tumbled about the room and melted into giggles. "Well, we could have guessed as much." Nana actually *winked* at him.

"No, I had another reason to return here before we head off to Hawaii." He looked down into her face. "But it's a surprise... so if Cinderella here will come with me, I have somewhere to take her."

She smiled. "Of course. Just let me fetch my glass slippers."

He hated to take his eyes off her to watch the road as he drove. "I've really missed you."

"Only a few more weeks!" Cara's voice was full of encouragement. "But I know. I can hardly wait."

He passed their intended location, knowing they had a few more minutes to kill before the appointment. He'd circle back.

"So... how is the desk work at the Agency suiting you?" There was a tinge of something unfamiliar in her tone as she asked that question. But what was it? Fear? Anxiety? Hope?

"I'd love to pass off some glib answer." He looked at her for a few seconds. "But I want our marriage to be entirely open and honest, and I'm not going to start hiding things now."

She nodded. "I agree – no secrets from each other." Then she stared intently at his face. "You hate it, don't you."

It wasn't a question.

He turned and drove slowly along a quiet road leading into the middle of nowhere underneath spreading oaks and magnolias.

Sitting at a desk in the underground building that housed the US branch of the top-secret I.C.E. Agency had turned out to be a lot harder... and more boring... than he'd envisioned.

He missed the thrill of being out in the middle of the action... running for his life. And the mountains of paperwork gave the Alps a run for their money.

"It's not unbearable, but I feel... stifled. Cooped up." They passed a small farm and saw a pinto pony trotting around a field, head cocked high, tail flowing in the wind.

"I guess I feel kind of like that little horse." He nodded his head in the direction of the pasture. "I was born to run free."

Born to serve. Born to protect. Born to be an intelligence agent fighting for my country, and all I hold dear.

He could see her swallow, her slim throat moving with the motion. "I know." And then Cara stretched out her hand and slipped it through his, leaving him one hand free to hold the wheel as they continued down the back road.

"Bryce... I understand the risks of becoming your wife. You're not... safe." She laughed and shook her head back and forth, drawing a deep breath as if to ward off tears. But they fell anyway as she spoke again. "Isn't that crazy? Because I never feel *safer* than when I'm with you."

He swallowed down the lump forming in his own throat as they cruised around, gradually following a circle back to their pre-planned target.

"God has everything under control." He told himself, as much as her. "And he works everything out according to his perfect plan. We don't have to be scared about what the future holds for us."

She nodded, eyes wide. "And..." She trailed off, then enfolded his hand inside both of hers. "What about your father?"

A terrible screeching noise shredded through the air and they were both thrown forward as the car jerked to a halt. It took him three long seconds to realize he had slammed on the brakes. Empty road stretched behind them and in front of them.

Cara stared at him, lips parted, stunned into silence.

First Blake, now you! What is it with everybody asking about my dad these days?! He struggled to maintain control, biting his lip.

"You're furious." She stroked his hand in hers, which sent a wave of peace washing over him again.

"I'm sorry, I'm sorry..." Where had the anger come from so suddenly? "I... it's just..." He looked out the window, unable to meet her gaze for a moment. "He's not a part of my life anymore."

He deserted me. Deserted the whole family. Just up and high-tailed it out of there with one cold, short note that he was leaving. I'm not going to go searching for him now.

"But he could be." The voice of his beloved broke through the bitter chant of pain and sorrow. He looked back to find her eyes on him. "My dad is *dead*. You can't get much farther away than that. I would give anything to be able to speak to him one last time." Her lower lip trembled.

"Oh, hon..." He looped his arm around her shoulders and she tipped her head against his shoulder.

Her voice drifted up to his ears. "I just think he should be told that you're getting married, that's all. Leave the rest up to him."

Indecision tugged him in two directions as he pushed the gas pedal and continued down the empty road. But then his insides settled into their proper positions again. "I'm sorry, but I can't. I'm not ready to see him again."

"All right." Cara sat up straight as they reached Main Street once more. "I'll leave the timing up to you. I'm content to wait if you are."

He smiled at her, hoping she wouldn't be able to see the agony inside of him. "Thanks, Carebear." The endearment earned him a smile.

It was then that he pulled up to the building. "Here we are!"

Cara's mouth dropped open. "The Banquet Hall?"

In front of them rose the Banquet Hall of Alvaton. The beautiful hall was the only thing the tiny town had going for it. They'd celebrated their engagement there with an elegant dinner. It was a gathering place for all sorts of events, from proms to... wedding ceremonies.

She looked at him.

"No, no, don't worry, this isn't an elopement." He laughed as he opened the door for her. "Your surprise is something else – dancing lessons!"

The birds chirped merrily in the trees outside Nana's house while they stood on the porch. "It was so sweet of you to take me dancing." Cara smiled up into her fiancé's face.

Bryce winked at her. "Well, I wanted to make sure we looked good together at the wedding reception."

"Oh, was that all?" She grinned.

"That… and I just had to see you again." He pulled her into a hug. "I have to go."

She sighed against him. "Okay. I'll miss you."

He let go of her and hopped back into his black mustang GT convertible. The top folded down and he started the motor with a throaty roar. He looked up and blew her an air kiss. "See you in Hawai'i!"

Turtle Bay resort was kissed with soft ocean breezes and bathed in warm sunshine when the appointed weekend finally arrived. Palm trees swayed above the lush, well-manicured landscape, and the sweet breath of tropical blossoms floated on the air. It was a perfect backdrop for a beautiful wedding.

But not until tomorrow. Penny reminded herself, rubbing her arms after a shiver wiggled through her. Her greatest fear was that she wouldn't be able to control herself at the wedding. Nightmarish scenarios plagued her… what if she started bawling at the altar or had a nervous breakdown walking down the aisle? She drew in a deep breath, making a conscious effort to relax. She and Cara reclined in buttery-smooth leather chairs waiting for their perfect pedicures to dry.

Riiiing! Cara's purse jingled. Cara leaned over and hoisted up her purse, plunging her hand inside and quickly locating her cell phone. Penny watched as her friend's face radiated utter delight.

"Hi." Cara sounded breathless, as if the air had all escaped from her lungs.

Penny waited, listening to the side of the conversation she could hear, although it was perfectly obvious from Cara's expression that only one special person could be on the other end of the line. No one but Bryce brought that particular sparkle into her eyes.

"We'll see you in a few minutes, then. I can't wait!" Cara eyed her wet toenails with a wrinkled nose, as if willing them to dry faster.

"Future hubby anxious to see you again?" Penny cringed at the hint of sarcasm that had speared into her voice.

Thankfully, Cara was in such a twitterpated state, she didn't notice. "He's meeting us here, in the salon." She gave a little bounce in her chair. "All the Reynolds family has arrived."

Wonderful. Now we get to meet the perfect in-laws. "How many of them are there again?" Penny reclined slightly in her chair as Cara began to recite a litany of names, starting with the immediate family and then chattering about the pair of cousins and their adorable children, who would be the flower girl and ring bearer.

"Bryce's grandparents are all deceased, and his father won't be coming to the ceremony." Cara's eyes darkened slightly in hue.

Before Penny could ask why Bryce's father wasn't coming to the wedding, and why she hadn't heard about that earlier, the door to the salon opened and a beaming Bryce came bounding towards them.

With a glad smile and laugh, Cara opened her arms wide. Bryce knelt beside her chair and hugged his bride-to-be.

Penny averted her eyes from the heart-shattering sight to see a huge pair of shoulders turn slightly to fit through the door. Set atop them was a head of thick chocolate-brown hair and a face that was all grin, until you noticed the eyes. Brown eyes, full of light, which immediately locked with hers.

He liked her. She could tell from the way one side of his mouth tilted up, revealing a killer dimple in his tanned cheek. But what did she have to fear? Nothing could make her forget… Mason. She lifted her chin slightly. There wouldn't be any problem avoiding this stranger.

"Penny, you know my brother, Blake." Bryce and Cara had moved apart, and now Bryce stretched out a hand in the direction of The Cute One.

Oh.

Avoiding him might be more difficult than previously thought. Yes, she *had* met this guy, at Cara's engagement dinner… but at the time her affections had been secretly engaged, with no freedom to focus on the man who'd been behind the camera, photographing it all.

"It's an honor to be in your presence again, Milady." A long, muscular arm swept in front of himself in a bow that would have been courtly in the 1700s but was hilariously grandiose when stuck in a modern setting.

A bubbly laugh came out of nowhere, nearly making her jump when she realized it was her own.

"Great to see you too, hotshot." *Whoops – did I just call him... oh no! Pile on more humor to save face!* "So are you guys here for your *man*icures?"

Both Bryce and Blake guffawed and giggles flowed from Cara.

Whew.

~*~

It was beyond sweet to see their two families mingling together around the side of the pool. His mother and cousins chatted with Cara's mom and grandma, while the little ring bearer and flower girl, twins named Andrew and Allison, frolicked in the shallow end. Bryce thought his heart might just burst from all the love pulsing through it... but miraculously, it kept on beating. A thread of conversation reached his ears. "... the *best* version is the '95 one with Colin Firth and Jennifer Ehle."

The girls, sitting on the pool's edge with their feet dangling in the water, were discussing *Pride & Prejudice* while Blake feigned disinterest. Well, he'd just mix things up a little. "I think Blake liked that one best too, didn't you, Blake? Of course, you've seen all of Bethany's Jane Austen movies..."

Before he could get anything else out, Blake lunged through the waist-high water and tackled him. Just before his head went underwater, he could hear the squeals of laughter pouring from the girls at Blake's 'secret' being revealed.

He slipped from Blake's grasp and came up, shaking the water from his eyes and laughing.

"Hey, man, you're messin' up my image!" Blake's half-whisper was accompanied with a frown and a slant of his gaze towards the girls.

"Your image. Huh." Then he noticed Blake's gaze lingering on Penny's smiling face. "Oh, your *image*. Right." He leaned closer to his brother's ear. "You *like* her."

"Yeah." Blake gritted the word between his teeth, pitched at a volume only Bryce could hear.

Oh. You really do *like her.* He'd have to lay off the heckling. "Sorry, dude."

Blake waved it off. "Nah, it's fine. But if it's storytelling you wanna do..." He wiggled his eyebrows and looked at the ladies. "There was that time when Bryce tried to give the cat a bath..."

CHAPTER TWO
Here Comes the Bride

Cara held the pure white gardenia blossom to her nose and breathed deeply of the sweet, rich fragrance. Her mom, Nana, Dawn, Bethany, and Penny were bustling around busily in the room behind her while she stood at the window in silent contemplation, wearing silk pajama pants and a button-up shirt with the word "BRIDE" on it in rhinestones. Out beyond the glass windowpane she could see half of the Y-shaped resort, with the ocean stretching to the horizon. The fabled North Shore of Oahu.

This is it. Oh God, am I doing the right thing?

Yes. The word washed through her in a soothing flow.

A slim arm slipped around her and Penny tucked her chin on top of her shoulder. "Bridal jitters?"

Cara smiled. "Just thinking." Her voice sounded soft and dreamy, an echo of her thoughts.

The bubbling of female conversation continued behind them. "Dawn, what do you think of these flowers?" Nana held up Penny's maid of honor bouquet. "Here, I'll take them. They look wonderful." Dawn took the flowers as Nana turned to help Bethany with her hair.

"I love how they've all grown so close... like real family." Cara whispered into Penny's ear with a backward glance over her shoulder at the women.

"Well, in a very short time, it'll be official. You *will* be family."
Penny gave a mock frown. "I'm jealous!"

Cara laughed. "Don't be jealous. You're already part of the
family, and *always* will be."

Penny's eyes widened as a soft gasp escaped her. "Seriously?"

Cara nodded. "You're stuck with us for good."

Mom appeared and tugged on her elbow. "Cara, come along,
it's time to get into your dress."

The prayer that he and Blake and Pastor Matt had prayed
together before the ceremony went straight to his heart and
settled there like a blanket of peace. Now Bryce stood at the
head of the aisle, feeling excitement growing inside of him as
the music changed into the wedding march. Their friends and
family waited with smiles on their faces, seated before him in
the decorated chapel. There was an almost holy atmosphere
with all the gauzy ribbon on the ends of the aisle and the white
flowers gleaming from every nook and corner.

The bridal procession began forming in the entryway of the airy
chapel, although from where he stood he couldn't see Cara yet.
Bethany and his good friend and fellow agent, Markdown, came
first. Bethany looked like a petite princess in her aquamarine
gown. Mark flashed him a grin, and his eyebrows disappeared
up underneath his long blonde bangs. Few people knew that
Mark's hair hid an ugly scar that he'd gotten while on a
particularly perilous mission. Bryce had been there when it
happened. Beth and Mark split at the top of the aisle and took
their places on either end of the front.

Penny and Blake walked down the aisle next, and he noticed that they *did* make a good-looking couple. Blake's chocolate brown hair blended with Penny's rich auburn tresses. They split and Blake slipped in between him and Mark, as Best Man, while Penny stood between Beth and the altar in the place of Maid of Honor.

Then adorable 4-year old Andrew walked down, tightly gripping the pillow with the rings as if determined to do his best. Bryce congratulated him as he reached the front with a whisper of "Great job, buddy." Andrew grinned as they looked up to see his twin sister Allison delicately scattering white rose petals down the path of the aisle, a pretty smile on her little face.

Bryce's heart pounded just like when he was running at top speed through the streets of Paris. *Here comes the bride.*

And then, there she was, escorted by his longtime friend, mentor, and boss, Benjamin Montrose, as Cara's father was deceased. Monty had become like a second father to her as well. Cara glided from the entryway and started her walk down the aisle. Her smile was almost blinding, her form clad in a satiny gown with subtle sparkle, and a truly radiant glow on her face that shone through the misty veil. Her long hair swirled in Rapunzel-length golden waves all the way down her back.

It was like beholding her anew for the very first time.

Cara felt as if she was walking on clouds, glad for Mr. Montrose's steadying arm, which kept her from slipping down and falling from the heavens. Bryce's whole face shone when he caught sight of her, making her heart leap inside.

She focused on each step, meanwhile keeping her gaze on Bryce's smile. She heard voices, and saw the pastor speaking, but everything sounded faraway until Montrose released her into Bryce's care and his strong, warm hand closed around hers. Penny held the precious bouquet of white roses and hibiscus, with a tiny portrait of her father, Dale Stephenson, tucked in the center.

Pastor Matt smiled down at the two of them. "I can't tell you how happy I am to stand here today with these two wonderful people in front of me." Out of the corner of her eye, Cara could see the small crowd nodding and smiling in response. The good pastor went on to talk about the beauty of love and marriage, weaving in the gospel message during his short speech. Then the time came to say their vows.

She gazed straight up into Bryce's eyes as he began to speak, reading from a piece of ivory paper that Blake handed him.

"Cara, I love you. Long ago you were just a hope and a prayer. On this special day, like a dream come true, the Lord Himself has answered that prayer. For today, Cara, you become my crowning joy. I thank God for the honor and blessing of going through life with you by my side. With our future shining bright before us, I will serve you, care for you, honor and protect you. I lay down my life for you, Cara, my friend, and my love."

His voice was warm and full of an intensity that said he meant what he was promising. Knowing that he truly would lay down his life for her, or in the call of duty as an intelligence agent serving their country, added even more weight to his words.

Cara drew in a shaky breath, silently praying for the strength to get through her vows without crying, and turned slightly to take the matching piece of ivory paper that Penny handed her.

"Bryce, I love you and I know you love me. I am confident that God has chosen you to be my husband. It is my prayer and desire that you will find in me the helpmeet God designed especially for you, and in confidence I will submit myself unto your headship as unto our Lord. Therefore, Bryce, I pledge to you my life as an obedient, faithful and loving wife. Where you go I will go, where you stay, I will stay, your people will be my people, and your God my God."

Bryce stroked the back of her hand with his thumb. She could tell from the tender look in his eyes that he was deeply moved by her words.

"Now for the rings." Pastor Matt nodded to Blake, who slipped the rings to both her and Bryce. Bryce looked her in the eye and slid the slim white-gold circlet onto her finger, nestling it against her engagement ring.

"With this ring, I thee wed."

Then she carefully slid the matching, slightly wider ring of white gold on to Bryce's long, lean finger.

"With this ring... I thee wed." She could feel the smile on her lips, springing there of its own accord.

Pastor Matt cleared his throat and they both looked up at him. "Bryce and Cara... do you promise to have and to hold each other from this day forward, for better or for worse, for richer, for poorer, in sickness and in health, to love and to cherish each other, until heaven and then forever?"

They smiled at each other, and then looked back to Pastor Matt and said in perfect unison "We do."

"Then I pronounce you man and wife." An enormous grin split the young pastor's face. "Bryce, you may kiss your bride."

Then her lips were claimed in a beautiful, gentle, soft-as-cream kiss.

Bryce opened his eyes to behold for the first time... his wife. Cara's eyes had never sparkled as brilliantly as they did now. "I love you." She mouthed the words silently. Their first kiss, *ever*, had been more amazing than he could ever have hoped. The waiting had been worth it.

Married. For real.

Wow.

The crowd clapped in approval, and Blake let loose with an earsplitting whistle. Tears were streaming down the maid of honor's face, and Bethany produced a tissue, apparently from thin air, and handed it to her, though she looked almost in need of it herself.

As they turned to face the crowd, he noticed faces here and there that stood out. His mom, beaming softly. Cara's grandmother and mom, both sobbing and laughing at the same time. Markdown's wife, Angelwing, who was also an old friend and fellow agent, grinning and giving him a thumbs-up. His cousin Melanie and her husband Thomas, waving to their children, the ring-bearer and flower girl. Monty, his boss, with an approving look on his brown, weathered face. Fellow agents studded the crowd as well... Shadowchaser, Cobalt, Quicksilver, Vixen, and many others who had saved his life a time or two. Just the presence of all these operatives had necessitated an invisible perimeter of top-level security.

Cara slipped her arm through his elbow before they proceeded back up the aisle, and for a moment he was transported back to the streets of Venice, where they had first strolled arm-in-arm down a sidewalk in the evening air. The mission had been thrown-together and fraught with danger, but in the midst of all the trouble, they found love. He, the hardcore agent, had fallen hard for the naïve graphic designer, his childhood best friend.

And now they were married.

Blake held out his hand towards Penny, and as she took it, he realized her whole form was trembling slightly. Her face looked a little frozen. He leaned close to whisper near her head. "Are you okay?"

She gave a short nod and smiled around at the crowd as they followed upon Bryce and Cara's swiftly retreating heels. But the smile looked forced, somehow. Odd.

"You sure?" They exited the chapel into the warm, beachy air, the rest of the wedding party following them out the door. The giggles of the ring bearer and flower girl mingled with Mark and Beth's congratulations to the wedded couple.

Penny looked up at him with eyes as blue as forget-me-nots. "Yes, I'm fine." She sniffed, looking away. "I almost feel like I'm losing her." The words came out as the lightest of whispers as she gazed out at the horizon.

He squeezed her slim hand in silent sympathy, earning a grateful glance from her just before they walked up to the bride and groom. "Congrats, you two!" He jubilantly pounded Bryce's back, then kissed Cara's hand.

Penny hugged Cara. "I am so happy for you!" Her voice rang with sincere enthusiasm.

The photographers waited to escort them and the rest of the families to a private beach location, where they would finish taking the wedding pictures while the guests made their way to the reception area in the gorgeous *Kuilima* Ballroom.

Penny turned away from Cara, her face hidden from everyone except him for just a split-second. The expression on her face stunned Blake. It wasn't happiness.

It was raw sorrow.

Cara was happy that her new husband had taken the time to show her how to dance earlier, for now everybody watched their first dance together as man and wife. Bryce waltzed her around the gleaming tiled dance floor with a gentle hand around her waist.

She caught whirling glimpses of the guest's faces, and every single one of them wore a smile.

"You're quiet." Bryce kept his voice low and soft, so that nobody could hear him but her.

Joy sparked through her again, in a nearly electrifying sensation. "My heart is too full for words." She snuck a quick glance towards her feet. "That, and I'm trying not to trip over myself."

He chuckled. "You're as light on your feet as a deer."

She could feel herself blushing at the compliment. "I had a good teacher."

Bryce nodded. "The dance instructor wasn't half bad."

She gazed directly into his eyes. "I was talking about you."

He grinned, and sent her out for a spin, before pulling her close once more. "Thanks."

"I never dreamed that you were an amazing dancer. That was an added perk in the deal."

A dimple showed in Bryce's half-smile. He dipped his head a little closer. "By the way, your dress is absolutely stunning."

Get ahold of yourself, Penny!

She knew Blake had seen her face outside the chapel. A perturbed wrinkle had creased his forehead. Now she would have some explaining to do.

Maybe it isn't such a good idea to not tell anyone about Mason. Maybe it'd be easier if someone knew. Keeping this secret might cost her more than spilling it out. She couldn't have people thinking she wasn't happy about Cara and Bryce getting married. *I* am *happy for them. It just reminds me of my own pain.*

"May I have this dance, milady?"

She was startled from her inner reverie by the cheerful voice of Blake, who held out his hand to her, palm up.

No! No, absolutely not. "Sure." *Why did I just say that? Well... there wasn't a good reason to say no.*

She tucked her hand into his and he led her to the dance floor. Bryce had already danced with his mother and sister, and Cara had danced with Blake and the other groomsman... now assorted couples filled the ballroom. The music had just shifted into something fun... some guy was singing about life giving him lemonade. Cara must have picked out that one. "I guess this would be a good time to tell you I can't dance."

He laughed. "Neither can I." A wink briefly interrupted his twinkling gaze.

"What?!" She was stunned into laughing along. "Then what are we doing?"

Blake slid his other arm around her back and held her hand in the air. "Faking it."

Penny could feel the grin spreading across her face as she followed his lead, stepping back and forth in time to the beat.

"Feeling better now?" his question was innocent and open, with no hint of judgment.

She looked up into his face, feeling a sinking sensation in her stomach, almost like falling to ground floor in an elevator. "I'm fine." She searched his eyes for suspicion or disgust, but none showed. Just that slight wrinkle in his brow. "I'm genuinely happy for them... this all just reminds me of something else that makes me sad." *Lame. So lame. I sound like an idiot.*

"Oh, I see." To her shock, he sounded like he understood. His forehead smoothed out again.

And then the song ended, the dancers finding their way back to their tables.

Disappointment streaked through her. "That was quick."

Blake looked around, seeming to take in the emptying dance floor. "Have time for another?"

"I do." *Oh, good grief. That sounded like a vow!*

Bethany squeezed his arm. "Bryce, I am so happy for you."

He smiled down at his sister. "Thanks, Bethy. I enjoyed that dance with you." Just then, a familiar face caught his eye. Shadowchaser stood nearby, looking like a plain, unobtrusive shadow himself. Trent was of average height, with an unremarkable face – perfect for a secret agent. Bryce often got ribbed by some of the other people in the Agency for being too tall and 'good-looking' for an agent. Often, it was best not to draw much attention.

"Hey Trent! Good to see you again, man." Bryce held out his hand for Trent's customary iron-grip handshake. Trent didn't disappoint.

"Hey Bryce." Trent's gaze flicked to Cara, who stood talking with her boss, Mr. Gungerson, and some of her coworkers that had made it to the wedding. One of them happened to be Freddie Donaldson, the man they had rescued in their previous mission. "Congratulations. She's lovely."

"That she is. Inside and out." He noticed Bethany quietly studying his friend. "Trent, have you met my sister? This is Bethany."

Beth smiled shyly and offered her hand. *Uh-oh.* But apparently, Trent held back on the iron for this particular handshake. He took Bethany's hand gently.

"Nice to meet you." Trent's nearly-black eyes grew warmer for a moment.

Huh. Interesting.

Bethany nodded, the ends of her deep-brown hair floating around her jawline. "Likewise." Her expression remained serene.

Trent looked towards the dance floor and opened his mouth, but before he could say anything…

"Trent!" A coppery blonde popped out of nowhere and yanked on Shadowchaser's arm. "You said we were going to dance the next one, and here you are just yammering!" She looked up. "Congrats, Bryce."

He tilted his head in a nod. "Thank you, Vicky." *Vixen, that is.* And a very apt codename it was.

"See you later." Trent managed to sputter before Vixen dragged him off.

Bethany looked after the two curiously, but explaining the complicated relationship between Trent and Vixen was more than he cared to attempt at the moment. He looked up to find Cara's eyes on him.

He had more pleasant things to think about right now. Like sampling the delicious tropical buffet, with his beloved at his side. And later... the honeymoon.

CHAPTER THREE

Trouble in Paradise

"It's so nice to just be *alone*." Cara looked up at her handsome husband. "No distractions, no disasters clamoring for your attention at the Agency, no well-meaning friends, no nothing. Just us."

The salty air caressed her face as they meandered slowly along the beach. In the days of their honeymoon that had slipped past so far, they'd ridden horses along the beach trails, gone mini-golfing, swam in the sea, dined on five-star island cuisine, read their Bibles together, and spent plenty of time alone in the luxurious hotel suite.

"Mmm." Bryce closed his eyes briefly. "Yeah. It's amazing." The setting sun cast a golden hue over his light-brown hair.

The waves were gentle this evening, stroking the shore rather than pounding it. They'd wandered far from most of the people along the beach, closer to a more untamed side of the bay. The strip of sand narrowed between the vegetation and the ocean.

Cara swung the sandals in her hand back and forth, enjoying the feel of bare toes against the powdery sand. Her other hand was safely enclosed in Bryce's grasp as they strolled.

"I don't want to think about 'real life' just yet." She noticed a huge luxury powerboat on the horizon, leisurely coming towards the shore. "That will intrude on this bliss soon enough.

Let's just take the next few precious days we have left, and savor them."

Bryce stopped walking and gently pulled her closer. "Agreed." He lowered his lips to hers in a warm kiss that sweetly lingered.

A thrashing in the underbrush behind them assaulted her ears, and they both whirled around to see men pouring out from among the trees, dressed head-to-toe in camouflage, faces hidden with black masks. One fired a warning shot into the air. They all carried menacing weapons, but she and her husband were unarmed.

Before they could even make a move, four men were grasping Bryce by the arms and one had a burly arm thrown around his neck. Two men clutched her in grips as strong as steel.

She screamed, her voice climbing so high her vocal cords nearly ripped, but there was no one to come to their aid. The nearest people were a sleeping elderly couple in lounge chairs, a good 100 yards away, with the resort and populated beach stretching behind them. No one else was even aware of what was happening.

Her gaze darted to Bryce's eyes, which met her own for a nanosecond, and in them she saw shock, anger, and something she'd never glimpsed there before.

Desperation.

She flung her beaded sandals farther up the beach, struggling.
"Let GO of me!" She yelled at her captors, but before the words
hit the air she knew they were useless.

Then a chugging, rushing sound approached from the sea. By
craning her neck, Cara could see a small boat pushing through
the water, manned by another man in camo. The men hauled
her and Bryce bodily across the sand and through the water,
hastily hurling them into the boat.

Bryce slipped one arm free and managed to land one solid
punch in the gut to one of their attackers, but the man only
grunted low in his throat. In the next instant, Bryce was held
captive once more, and this time the men bound his arms
behind his back with thick black tape.

Within a few seconds, they were motoring out from the shore
again, now headed towards the luxury cruiser Cara had noticed
earlier. She jerked her gaze back to her husband. Bryce's chest
heaved under his T-shirt and his chiseled jaw was clenched
tight, but he remained silent. His eyes never stopped moving,
from her, to the boat, to the men, to the water. She could tell
he was assessing the situation in his mind. She didn't have to be
an agent to know what he was thinking. It was hopeless.

They reached the boat and were pulled into it by even more
men. The rest of their captors clambered up behind them on
their own, tying the small boat to the side of the cruiser. She
and Bryce were half-carried to the upper section of the boat.

One of the men pulled a door open in the sleek wood floor,
revealing narrow ladder-like stairs that led to the hold below.

The men holding Bryce shoved him towards the opening. Bryce started down the stairs, but then the man he'd punched earlier shoved him again. Bryce lost his footing and fell the rest of the way down the seven steps.

Meanwhile, the men holding her arms let go. She instantly clambered down next to her husband. "Bryce!" She knelt next to him and cupped his cheek in her hand. He'd banged it against the stair railing.

He looked at her, and the anger in his eyes softened for a second. "I'm ok." He kept his voice low, almost to a whisper.

No, you're not! But she didn't reply audibly. She took a second to look at their surroundings. They'd landed on the thin carpeting of the hold, in between a shiny galley kitchen in the stern of the boat and a posh seating area in the middle. An open doorway looked like it led to a bedroom in the bow.

But apparently they weren't to wait on the floor. Three men followed them down the steps and pushed them towards the front of the boat. Two of them frisked Bryce, and confiscated his phone from his pants pocket. The third man merely held out his hand towards her.

"Your phone." He demanded.

Her husband nodded, so she quickly complied, pulling her smartphone from her pocket and surrendering it.

The men forced them into the small bedroom, Bryce again being pushed to the floor by the man who'd been punched. The men slammed and locked the door behind them.

Thin strips of window let in the fading sun, and tiny accent lights shone in all three corners of the room, reflecting off the gleaming hardwood cabinets. Cara helped Bryce to his feet and they sank onto the plush bed, knocking aside some of the designer-print pillows. It wasn't until then that Cara realized her heart was pounding so hard it almost seemed to be booming its way out of her chest.

She released an anguished sigh, wrapping her arms around Bryce. "What just happened?"

He grunted. "No idea." He tilted his mouth against her ear and murmured. "Shh. They might be listening."

She shuddered, and tightened her grip on him. Then she let go and reached for his bound hands, trying to pull off some of the tape.

Bryce shook his head. "No use. Stuff's like duct tape on steroids."

"Ugh." He was right. She couldn't break or peel away the tape. It would have to be cut. A brief scan of the room revealed there was nothing remotely sharp enough.

She put her lips close to his ear. "Do you have anything-?"

"Shh." He cut her off with a short shake of his head.

Drat. She'd been hoping he had a knife concealed on him. Now the situation was critical.

God, please help us!

Blake trailed his finger along the bookshelf, scanning the titles. One caught his eye and he pulled it from the shelf to peruse its contents. A voice over a loudspeaker arrested him mid-page. *"The library will be closing in fifteen minutes."*

His head jerked upright and he tucked the book underneath his arm. He only had fifteen minutes and he was going to make the most of each one. He wove his way out of the bookshelves and headed for the front desk. Once there, he cleared his throat, and the middle-aged librarian looked up, her head of salt-and-pepper curls bouncing.

"Yes, how can I help you?" Her voice was husky, even a little gravelly. Not the woman's voice he'd just heard over the loudspeaker, which was sweet and silky-smooth.

"The young lady who just spoke over the loudspeaker... where is she?"

"Oh, that's one of our junior librarians."

"Could I possibly speak with her?"

With a reluctant sigh, she closed the book she'd been reading and walked into the back area of the library.

Blake laid the book he'd been carrying on the counter and waited. In a few seconds, a young woman appeared in the doorway. He nearly laughed out loud at the look of surprise that washed over the pretty face covered with a sprinkling of freckles.

"Blake?"

I thought I recognized her voice. "Hello, miss. I was wondering if I could check out this book." He thumped the book for emphasis.

She still stared at him, stunned, but he couldn't yet tell if she was pleased to see him or not. "What are you doing here?"

He grinned. "I've moved here. I live in Peachtree City now."

Comprehension lit her eyes. "Oh." The word was short, but a smile tugged at her full lips.

"The library will be closing in ten minutes." This time it was the hint-of-gravel voice of the older librarian who announced the message. A few people walked up, waiting in line behind Blake at the library desk.

Penny darted forward with the quickness of a minnow. "I'll check out your book." She paused when she caught sight of the rainbow-colored cover. "The LEGO Ideas Book: Unlock Your Imagination...?" She slanted her gaze up to him, a quizzical quirk to her pale eyebrows.

"I thought it might give me some fresh inspiration."

"You like Legos?"

"I mostly build castles. Big ones." He spread out his hands to give her an approximate idea of the size of them.

Her eyebrows rose. "Oh! Wow." She tilted her head. "So... do you have a library card?"

Oops. "Uh, no... I guess I forgot about that. I only have my Colorado library card."

A tubby blonde lady trotted out from the back area and began checking out the other waiting people.

Penny bit her lip. "Well," Her gaze flicked to the orange wristwatch on her arm, "I'll do my best to get you out of here on time."

"Sounds great. Thanks." He watched in admiration as Penny's fingers whirled over the computer keys and she clicked the mouse in rapid succession.

"Here you are!" She slipped him a brand-new library card with a flourish, eyes glinting with triumph. "Now let me help you check out this book." Penny scanned the barcode on the back of the LEGO book and handed it to him. "Have a good evening."

"You too." He half-turned away, but turned back. "So... would you like to go out for coffee in a few minutes? When you close?"

She hesitated for a moment, nodded. "Sure." She bit her lip again before adding "I'll meet you by the fountain out front."

When Penny walked out into the humid Georgia June evening, Blake was waiting by the huge fountain for her. It clinked and clanked, water trickling from tilting silver platforms in the center of a large round pool. Penny thought it ugly, but it held a certain fascination. However, it didn't compare with her curiosity about Blake.

Why is he here?

He turned and smiled as she approached. "So where's the nearest Starbucks from here?"

"Not far. I can show you."

"Shall we take my car or yours?" He looked around the parking lot as if wondering which vehicle was hers.

She flipped her hair over her shoulder. "I drove my golf cart." She pointed it out, parked in the far downhill corner of the lot.

He laughed and shook his head. "I still can't get used to seeing all the golf carts and golf cart paths around here. It's so cool."

They agreed to take Blake's navy-blue SUV, and he opened the passenger door for her.

He settled into the driver's seat as if quite at home, then smoothly wheeled them out of the parking lot. She gave him directions and they were soon walking into the Starbucks.

The rich smell of coffee embraced the air, with undertones of freshly baked pastries and an oriental hint of tea leaves. It was crowded, but Penny liked the feel of anonymity it gave them. They were just two more in a throng.

They stuck to a comfortable silence while waiting in line, then found an unclaimed table for two near a window.

"So..." Penny tasted her *Tazo* chai tea latte. "What brings you to Peachtree City?"

Blake finished swallowing his sip of Mocha Cookie Crumble Frappuccino before answering her. "My job. I had a good position working with a realtor in Colorado, an old friend of our family..." He tilted his head to one side, and a wistful expression crossed his face. "But he's like 65, so he decided to retire. I can't blame him at all. But I figured it was time for me to move on too... the real estate market out there is just drying up."

Penny savored the taste of the chai in another long sip as she listened, noticing that Blake's eyes were the same soft brown as the milk-chocolate chips in his mocha.

"I looked around the country for a better area to work in... and I liked this option best. We lived in Georgia when I was younger, and I liked it. Plus the real estate in the suburbs around Atlanta is on the upswing." Blake took another sip. "So I got a job working for the Century 21 office. I'm renting an apartment for now." He shrugged, and a twinkle sparkled in his eyes. "I'm just seeing it as a grand adventure."

"Wow." *He's moved here. My word. Now what?* "Did Cara know you were moving here? She never said anything about it." The chai latte seemed to have lost some of its flavor. Either that or her taste buds had gone numb.

He chuckled, an extremely attractive sound. "I think she was busy with wedding plans."

Cara! She knew! And she never dropped the merest hint! If the girl wasn't on her honeymoon, Penny would have called to give her a piece of her mind about this surprise.

"So you've been planning this for a while, then. Okay." *He didn't move here just for... my sake.* She should have been relieved, and she was... but then where was that bitter taste of disappointment coming from?

Blake nodded – an exuberant motion. "Yeah. I'm kind of excited about it... I feel like I have a chance to stretch my wings a little." He looked out the window, towards the streetlights illuminating the parking lot. "I *am* going to miss my mom and sister though." He sighed, and what looked like a hint of worry seeped into his face. "I'm hoping they'll be okay without me."

"Living on your own without a man around isn't *that* bad." Penny shrugged, aiming for nonchalance. "They'll be fine."

Blake squinted for a second, studying her, as if he didn't quite know what to make of that remark. Then he leaned back in his chair with a casual smile. "I've been talking about myself for a while. Tell me about you."

Woah. Blake was taken aback by how fast her face closed once he made that innocent suggestion. *This gal's got secrets.* But what were they? Meanwhile, he'd better lighten the atmosphere. "Nothing deep. Just stuff you like, hobbies, your opinions on the world at large…" He trailed off, seeing relief melt her tense features.

"Oh." She laughed a short, slightly nervous laugh, and then began to name off her favorite movies, and chatter about her favorite books. Penny obviously liked things with a touch of whimsy. She was in the middle of describing how much more wonderful the original Winnie the Pooh books were compared to the animated movies when she happened to shift her feet underneath the tiny table, bumping into his sneakers.

Her freckles faded into her skin as she flushed pink. "I'm sorry."

"No prob." She was treating it like it was a big deal, but he wouldn't… It wasn't. Was it?

It was then that she lifted her cup again and apparently noticed she'd finished her latte. She whipped out the orange wristwatch. "Oh my gosh!" She squealed. "9:45?"

He consulted the time on his phone. "Yup. So it is. Time flies when you're having-"

"I've got to get home!" She froze, as if realizing she'd interrupted him. "I'm sorry-"

"Penny, it's okay." He involuntarily reached for her hand, but she jerked it away and folded her hands in her lap. Her eyes stared at him, huge blue pools of fear.

Ouch. Everything was obviously not okay. He could feel his eyebrows climbing up in surprised arches.

She closed her eyes and took a deep breath. When she opened them again, she looked calmer. "I apologize that I'm so uptight. It's been a tough day, a lot of things went askew at work."

She gazed straight into his eyes. "And I don't think you're a creep. Not at all." She blushed again, but seemed determined to press on, increasing the pace of her words. "I just have my own issues concerning guys. I have a lot of baggage I've never told anyone about."

"Ohhh, I understand now." He rolled his shoulders back, realizing he'd tensed up. "I can handle that." *As long as you don't think I'm a creep.* He felt pleased at the friendly warmth he'd managed to infuse into his voice.

Her voice dropped low and soft when she spoke next. "Really?" Now *her* eyebrows were arching.

"Really." He stood up and tucked his hands into his pockets so he wouldn't accidentally reach for hers again. "Now let's get you home."

The only problem with getting Penny home was that when they got back to her golf cart, it was dead. Good thing he'd waited to make sure she'd be all right. The library parking lot was empty except for them.

"No!" Penny wailed, "You can't be dead! Not you too!" She tried the key again, with a panicky jerk of her wrist, but the engine wouldn't even turn over. She leaned her forehead on the steering wheel, her waves of red hair falling to hide her face.

"Aw, Penny, I'm sorry." *Poor thing. The last thing she needed was this...*

"This has *not* been a good day." The words floated up from somewhere beneath her auburn tresses. Then she jerked her head up. "I mean, aside from the coffee. I'm not saying that wasn't nice."

He held back a chuckle. "Don't worry, I'll take you home. You can call somebody to come and tow it."

Penny blinked, relief dawning in her eyes. "Thank you."

Bryce rolled his neck, trying to work out the crick developing in it. Three hours. That's at least how long they had been sitting there in the bedroom, while the boat rumbled below them, traveling through the ocean to who knows where. The light outside the window had completely vanished, and only the dim accent lights kept them from plunging into utter darkness. His hands were numb from being strapped behind his back with the XPLO-Tape.

51

Cara stirred beside him. She'd drifted into a catnap, leaning against him. How she could be relaxed enough to even half-sleep right now was a mystery to him. Her eyes, still murky with sleep, found his face. "Hey."

"Before you ask, nope... it wasn't a dream. We were abducted right off the beach." *Why didn't I have my gun on me?* Well, if he'd had his gun... he still couldn't have done much about all those men. But it hurt in so many ways that he'd been caught unawares.

"Oh drat." She ran her hand over her head, smoothing the hair tucked up in a bun. "I *was* hoping I'd dreamt that part." She slipped an arm around him and half-hid her face against him.

The door handle jiggled, and then swung open with a bang. In the brightly lit doorway, there stood a man he'd never seen before. He could have been a ranch hand, were it not for the aura of raw power and authority hanging around him. The man was dressed in jeans, leather cowboy boots, a leather jacket, and a ten-gallon hat that he wore like it was a crown.

"G'day mates. Bryce Reynolds... we meet at last." The guy had a twangy Aussie accent coming from between two lips held in a perpetual cruel twist. Cold, dark eyes pierced from a deeply lined, weathered face.

Cara felt her muscles freezing as she huddled next to Bryce, staring at this sudden apparition.

"You know, I expected more from you, Reynolds. For bein' a secret agent, or whatever it is that you ah, it was surprisingly simple to capture you."

Bryce stayed motionless except for the unbridled fury that flickered in his eyes.

"Ah suppose you're wonderin' what you're doin' heah." He leaned casually against the doorway. "I had a bone to pick with you, ya see. You put an end to the life of someone I deahly loved."

Cara watched Bryce's eyebrows lower and his eyes narrow. She could tell he didn't know what this man was talking about.

"That's right. You killed my brothah." The man's eyes grew even colder in pure hatred.

"His name?" Bryce's question zinged out and sizzled on the air.

"Of course. You've killed so many people it's hahd for you to remembah them all." He tipped his head as if being gracious. "I'll enlighten you." He pushed away from the door and took a menacing step closer. "His name was Jack, and you shot him down in a pizza pahlah. Three yeahs ago."

One of Bryce's eyebrows cocked up, but other than that he was still motionless. "Your name?"

"Hmm. Well, when you're goin' to die, Ah suppose you deserve to know the name of your enemy. The name's Cooper Farnsworth." His eyes briefly flicked to her. "Oh yeah, little lady, you heard me. You're goin' to die." His thumb jerked from her to Bryce. "You and him both."

Lord, protect us from this madman. HELP!

Bryce's jaw clenched, and she could feel the muscles rippling in his shoulder next to her. If his hands hadn't been bound behind him, she'd be concerned about the madman's health, but as it was, there wasn't much they could do. Besides, their foes were the ones with the guns.

Cooper snapped his fingers in a sudden, unexpected motion, and five men passed through the doorway and pulled them to their feet. Dread engulfed her as soon as she lost contact with her husband, but she refused to let it show on her face. Cooper might see it.

They made the expedition back through the lavishly furnished boat again, up the ladder-stairs, and onto the deck, where they were ordered into the smaller boat again. Cara clung to Bryce's side again. Gone was the Turtle Bay Resort and anything remotely familiar. They were idling near a narrow beach edged with rough jungle. The night was dark upon them but the moon gave some intermittent light between the clouds.

The last one onto the smaller boat was Cooper himself. He nodded to the helmsman, and they moved for the shore.

"You're hahd to find out about, Mistah Reynolds. Best I could come up with was that you worked 'for the government'." A sneer twisted his face even more into a cruel slant. "My guess is FBI. But that doesn't mattah now. The plan is already in motion. Your beloved US of A will be blown to bits. Payback for Jack."

Could this man be any worse? She had never felt such loathing.

The boat drew closer to the land. "Welcome to your final restin' place. The island of death."

The WHAT?

"You have exactly two weeks to slowly stahve to death, if you last that long. With no food and no wahtah, it shouldn't even take that long, but Ah don't want have to kill you myself." He held his head high like a proud stallion. "But if it comes down to that, Ah surely will. If Ah return to find you still alive, Ah'll kill the both of ya."

The prow of the boat dug into the sand, and Cooper signaled to his men with a jerk of his hand. The men lifted Bryce and threw him out of the boat, into the shallow water.

She leaped down next to him before she could be thrown likewise. The waves soaked both of them in seconds as she and Bryce struggled to their feet in the churning sand. They slogged up the beach, Cara half expecting to be shot in the back before they made it to dry land. But no bullets came.

Just before they reached the fringe of jungle, Cooper's voice floated through the darkness. "Remembah, I'll be back..."

In the darkening night, lit only by the lamp in the window and the winking yard lights lining the pathway to the front door, Penny's teeny-tiny house looked as if it had grown there, like a mushroom, rather than being built.

Penny hung her purse over her shoulder, but Blake opened the car door for her before she could even reach for the handle. He gave her a cheeky grin, as if pleased at his success at once again being the gentleman. "Sweet little place you've got here."

He'd parked on the paved driveway that divided the modest yard in half. Penny was thankful for the dark, which hid the fact that she needed to lug out the push-mower and cut the grass again. She sent a glare towards her car, which seemed to be waiting smugly underneath the overhang of the one-car carport. She preferred the golf cart, but it had failed her in her hour of need.

She trotted towards the front door. "Come on, I'll introduce you to Dot and Tulip."

Blake nodded and quickly fell into step with her. "Roommates?"

"No!" The word came out cloaked in giggles. "You'll see."

She unlocked the door and turned on the lamp beside the door, adding more light to the snug room, and closed the door behind them. "Dottie?"

Within seconds, a fluffy bit of something was winding around her legs and mewing.

"Hey baby." She picked up her friendly kitten and presented Dot's adorable face to Blake.

He visibly softened. "Aw, I love kittens." He held out his hands and little Dot leaped into them and batted a paw at the buttons on his shirt.

Blake laughed. "I think she likes me." He rubbed a finger under Dot's chin, which instantly won him her kitten's adoration. "So who's Tulip?"

Penny moved to the cage in the corner of the room and pulled off the silk cover. "He's my canary."

Tulip blinked and proceeded to break into warbling song. To her surprise, the dull ache that always poured through her at the sound was almost nonexistent.

Blake listened for a moment, eyes wide. "Wow." He eyed the kitten in his arms. "So do Dot and Tulip act like Sylvester and Tweety Bird, or do they get along?"

Penny replaced Tulip's cover carefully, feeling almost like a mother putting her child to bed. He stopped singing and went back to sleep. "So far, we haven't had any problems, and I intend to keep it that way. But if there were, poor little Dot would have to leave... I've had Tulip for ages, and I only just got her. But she's been a good girl."

Dot wiggled, so Blake set her down again, and the kitten made her way over to Penny by way of sneaking under the legs of the coffee table.

"Well, I'd offer you coffee, but we just had some..."

But Blake shook his head. "Oh, no, thanks, but I should be going, I've kept you out late as it is." He took a tentative step towards her. "However..."

She felt as if something drew her towards him, and found herself taking a step closer to him. "Yes?"

"How about dinner tomorrow?" Hope lit his face. "We could eat at my place, or go out somewhere."

No, no... well...- "All right. That would be nice."

"Great!" He looked so eager and happy, she was glad she'd agreed.

Blake wrote his address and phone number on the notepad she kept on the end table in the living room. "There you go." He clicked the pen closed and laid it next to the paper again.

Their eyes met. Penny swallowed. "Thanks for taking me home. I don't know how I'd have gotten back otherwise."

"Really, it was the least I could do. I'm so sorry about your golf cart." He reached out his hand as if to shake hers, but then pulled back, and they both laughed awkwardly.

That was embarrassing. "Thanks again."

"No problem." And then he'd slipped out the door.

She plopped down on the old loveseat in front of the window and watched as he got into his car. He spied her in the window and waved before backing out of the driveway.

She waved back. Then she gasped out loud at the sharp feeling of being so incredibly alone. Again.

Well, at least we're alone again. Cara gulped in a big breath of air, and huddled next to Bryce along the trunk of a coconut palm. They listened to the sound of the small boat sailing away from them through the night. At last the only thing they could hear was the crashing of the waves on the shore and the rustling of the palm leaves in the wind.

"Honey, they didn't kill us. We're still alive!" Hope sent a shaft of warmth through her.

"Yeah. We're alive, at least. Now, let's get my hands free." His voice was grim, but he sounded calm enough.

"How?"

"They missed my ultra-light Swiss army knife. It's sewn into a secret pocket in my pants leg."

She almost choked on her gasp. "You have a knife?!"

"If you'll kindly get it out for me, yep."

"Where is it?!"

"Right leg, just above the knee. You might have to roll up the pant leg and rip it out from the underside."

She set to work, pulling along the seam, trying to work the stitches loose. Her fingertips ached after a few tries, but she kept at it, and felt the sturdy fabric give way. "I should have known you wouldn't be caught without anything on you. Too bad you didn't have your gun."

He shook his head. "Even if I'd had it, we were badly outnumbered and they had the element of surprise." For a second, it almost sounded as if he was gritting his teeth. "They caught me *off guard*."

The opening was almost large enough to work the compact knife through. "Bryce, what did he mean about you killing his brother?"

Her husband leaned his head back against the tree trunk. "That was my first mission... the first time I ended up shooting a man. He opened fire on me first."

"I believe you."

"There was nothing else I could do." A short pause. "He hit his head on something sharp, and died."

"Mmm-hmm." She could sense that it hurt him to talk about it. "Did it really happen in a *pizza parlor*?"

That brought a short chuckle from him. "Yeah." He began telling her the whole story.

She particularly enjoyed the description of his undercover getup. "You. In saggy jeans. No... way..."

He snorted. "The things I do for this job." He finished relating the facts as she worked the knife from the pants leg. "...And then, after we got Habrin Merkochaz into custody, Monty gave me my code name."

She was fascinated. "So that's when you got code-named Ashburn?!" Then she felt the small smoothness of the Swiss army knife pop into her hand. "I got it!"

"Atta girl." She could hear the love and pride in his voice. "Open it."

She had to move into a patch of moonlight to be able to see the knife. It resembled a Swiss army knife, but was lighter, longer, and thinner, and the whole thing actually flexed a little bit in her hand when she pressed it... almost like a pair of glasses frames she'd seen. Flexible metal, it would be difficult to detect in the pocket if you didn't know it was there. Cara quickly pulled out what looked like the biggest blade in the knife. "Here, move into the light."

Bryce turned and scooted backwards into the moonlight, and she began sawing through the horrid black tape.

"Cut with the grain, up, away from my hands."

She did as instructed, and in a few moments she'd managed to rip apart the bonds holding his arms behind his back. Bryce swung his arms around and rolled his shoulders with a sigh of relief.

"Great, but we'll still have to rip the tape off your arms." She could see that strips of it stuck to him all the way up to his elbows.

He held out his arms. "Just do it. My hands are numb."

She let out a cry of horror. "Oh, Bryce!" She clasped his hands in hers and brought them to her lips, kissing his fingers. "Your poor hands!" She rubbed them, hoping to restore the feeling.

He gently tugged them away. "First get the tape off. If it's what I think it is, it's poisonous."

A gasp of shock stole her breath before she drew it back in. "OH my-" She ripped away, now frantic to tear the tape off. Low grunts from Bryce were the only indication of how much it hurt him.

"There! Last one!" She helped him to his feet and they washed off his arms and her hands in the salt water – then scrubbed them in the sand until her skin tingled.

"Antiseptic would have been better, but I hope that'll do the trick." Bryce led her back up the beach under the shelter of the trees.

She slipped her arms around him. "I'm so thankful you're all right."

Bryce tugged her into his lap and held her as they sat there in the sand. She'd never felt so safe, resting her head against his chest.

"Lord, we come to you now, thanking you for preserving our lives." He began to pray, and she joined in. They lifted up their praise and thanks to Him, and then asked for continued protection and guidance.

"Okay, Sugar. Let's try to get some sleep, and we'll further assess the situation in the morning." Bryce scooped aside the sand, sculpting a comfortable place for them to rest.

She loved it when he called her 'Sugar'. "Spoken like a true agent."

He chuckled. "Yeah." A few heartbeats passed. "Hey, thanks for staying positive. If we're gonna make it, the most important thing is attitude."

"Of course we'll make it!" They settled into silence, listening to waves along the shore, and the rustling of the breeze in the palm leaves.

...won't we?

CHAPTER FOUR

Secrets in Sydney

Greg felt his unease transfer into the horse beneath him, and it skittered side-to-side in nervousness.

"Whoa." He soothed, slapping its neck twice.

He looked up at the hills on the horizon. The rolling grassy slopes were dotted with patchy brush, Acacia trees providing scant shade from the already-blistering sun. Dust clouded the dry air.

Cattle mustering was the toughest part of running a station in the outback. Greg and the other cowboys were just getting started for the day, and he was already looking forward to a pot of beans simmered over an open flame for a hearty midday meal.

The boss wouldn't be joining them – in fact, he'd be flying down to Sydney, accompanying his wife to the famous Australian ballet. Everyone breathed a little easier without Cooper's stifling presence... no one more than Greg, what with the secrets he was shouldering.

He spurred his horse to catch a cow that made a break for freedom. "Not today, you bugger!" He and his steed chased the unwilling bovine back into the herd.

Greg had spent some long years on this Australian cattle ranch – or 'station', as they referred to them in Oz. It was both haven and prison for him. A hiding place from those who sought to destroy him... and an arena where he constantly had to watch his back and search for tidbits of information.

What could Cooper be doing in Sydney? He wasn't only going there to enjoy the performances of the ballet dancers in the world-renowned Sydney Theater, for sure. That was his wife's doing.

Something didn't smell right, and it wasn't the scent of hardworking horseflesh. Good thing he'd taken a chance and slipped a bug into Cooper's perpetually-worn cowboy hat. Fortunately for Greg, Cooper's wife always made him remove it for supper. He seized that moment while the hat was on the stand in the hallway to hide the listening device between the hatband and the soft leather.

Later that night he'd check the recording on the laptop hidden in his private quarters. As foreman, he had that privilege, and didn't bunk with the other jacks – temporary employees – in the bunkhouse.

We'll hear what you're up to, 'mate'. And I'll wager it isn't fun and games.

Bryce awoke to the realization that he was lying in the sand, on a beach... and it all came rushing back. *Left for dead. Pssh. We'll see about that.* He would foster that feeling of defiance. The defiant survived despite the odds.

The freshly risen sun cast gentle beams of light onto the face of his wife. She slept still, blissfully unaware for a little longer than he. *My wife.* The newness of it still caught him by surprise, and for a few seconds, he was turned to pudding, melted ice cream, liquefied by sheer gratitude.

Speaking of liquid – he was parched. They needed water, and soon. Dehydration would be their greatest enemy in the fight for life.

"Cara." He touched her cheek, and her eyelids fluttered open.

"…Hey, handsome." She closed her eyes again, smiled, and drew a deep, awakening breath.

"I hate to wake you up, but we need to get going. We've gotta find fresh water, and I think we may be able to collect some morning dew before it evaporates." He picked up half of a coconut shell to serve as a bowl.

Her eyes opened wide. "Right. That's important." She sat up straight and rubbed her face, blinking.

He stood and helped her to her feet, and they set off through the jungle. It was slow going, as both of them were barefoot and the undergrowth harbored the unfriendliest of sharp, rough textures. Sticks and branches and rocks lay concealed beneath the sandy soil.

But soon enough, they reached a clearing of wispy grass still shaded from the sunlight – and tiny drops of dew clung to the green blades.

"Oh!" Cara seemed about to dart out into the clearing, but he caught her wrist just in time, pulling her close.

"Stop!" He pointed to a thin rope, stretched taut across their path.

Cara froze.

He gripped a fallen palm stalk, reached out and tapped the string. Nothing happened. He pushed a little harder, and- "WHOOSH" – down from the treetop canopy, a stake with many blades attached came swinging and cut straight through the empty air in front of them.

Cara screamed, digging her fingers into the fabric of his shirt.

The malicious weapon swung to a stop, dangling like a corpse at the gallows.

He stared at it, horrified, as it turned slowly on the rope.

"Where did that come from?!" Cara's voice shredded the silence.

He swallowed. "More importantly, *who* did that come from?"

They looked at each other. He held her shoulders and drew out his next words. "We...need...to...be...*extremely*...careful."

"No kidding!" Cara's eyes were round as marbles. "This whole island could be booby-trapped!"

He clenched his jaw. "I won't let you get hurt." He stroked her hair, then released her and reached up to the bladed stake. He dismantled it, using his pocket knife to cut the larger knives from where they'd been tied together with twine.

Once he'd stacked the blades nearby and checked out the area, he turned his attention back to the task at hand – finding water.

As the least necessary piece of clothing between the two of them, Cara's soft cotton "cardi-wrap" was sacrificed. She gave it up willingly, even though he knew she loved the garment. They ripped it into four pieces and he tied them around their ankles.

"Walk through the grass, slowly, and let the rags soak up as much moisture as possible." He demonstrated.

His wife watched carefully. "Okay." She gingerly took two steps. "Hey, this actually feels delightful."

He smiled at the expression of pleasure on her face. She'd recovered from the swinging-knives scare. "I've heard this is how native aborigines gather several gallons of water in the mornings."

She looked over at him, eyes full of mirth. "You don't say."

"Yup. I think this is working, my rags already feel wet." Drops of water were even gathering on his legs.

"Woohoo! Mine too." Cara pumped the air with a slim fist, swishing her feet around in circles.

After several trips around the patch of grass and subsequent wringings of the rags into the coconut shell, they came up with enough water for each of them to drink several long swallows.

"You, sir, are a genius." Cara wiped a stray drop of water from her chin and sucked her finger. Every drop was worth its weight in gold at this point.

He chuckled. "Come here." They shared a triumphant kiss of victory. *One battle down, one war to go.*

When she pulled away, Cara's eyebrows curved up in a slightly mournful expression and her stomach growled. "Now... what to eat for breakfast?"

Cooper swallowed the yawn of boredom that threatened to embarrass him.

Ballet. Ugh. He could hardly stomach the sight of all the glittering people in tights and tutus gallivanting around like grasshoppers and whirling like tops. No matter that the setting was the opulent and grandiose great room of the Sydney Theater. The glowing lights and rosy-hued interior put the stage in center focus, while the balconies lined the walls up to the soaring ceiling.

He did, however, enjoy the story of the Swan Lake ballet. The black swan was used as a tool by the evil Von Rothbart to destroy the two lovers – dreaming Prince and delicate Odette. Watching the *pas de deux* of the black swan and the prince inspired him. *That's what I'll name the submarine. The Black Swan.* Elegant but deadly.

Veronica sat on the edge of her red velvet seat next to him, gazing raptly at the dancers. Marrying her had been the smartest decision he'd made, for when her daddy was called home to gloryland, she inherited 20,000 acres of fertile land and 2,000 head of cattle along with it... adding to his holdings considerably. She wasn't half bad to look at – a veritable Barbie doll with an Australian accent. She was a stunner tonight in her metallic purple gown, dripping with diamonds and heavy makeup.

Tonight's performance – a dose of 'real culture' – would keep her satisfied for months, so the significant blow to his checkbook was more than worth it.

He doubted she'd even notice his brief departure, what with the way she kept her baby blues glued to the stage, but he leaned in to whisper in her ear regardless.

"I'll be right back, dahlin'." He nearly gagged on the whiff of her dark, sultry perfume as he picked up the ostrich-leather briefcase.

A brief nod of her delicate chin was all the recognition his words received. So he rose, crept soundlessly from their luxurious theater box and arrived minutes later at the prearranged location – the men's restroom. Empty, since the performances were all mid-swing.

He was first to arrive, so he waited before one of the mirrors until the door creaked and his contact entered, steps echoing. The sounds sent chills down his left arm. Cooper looked up, and saw the man behind him in the reflection of the glass.

Nebo's eyes were mere slits in his deeply lined brown face, and his snaggle-toothed grimace made babies cry from the sheer evil. "Do you have it?"

"No, Ah came all this way and flew in mah helicopter and then private plane for hours – but didn't bother to bring the money." He turned to face the man, disgust pulsing through his core.

The sarcasm was lost on Nebo, whose expression remained deadpan. He waited, silent, for Cooper to make the next move.

"Yes, Ah brought it." But before he handed over the briefcase stuffed with Australian dollars, he demanded to know if his 'gift' had been acquired.

Nebo answered in the affirmative, providing satisfactory details.

Pleased, Cooper at last placed the smooth leather case in the hands of the fervent terrorist, and slipped back to his wife's side. Only a few more hours of this performance, and they could fly home more swiftly than those winged swans.

Soon, my perfect plan will have the weapon it requires. All I have to do is wait for the delivery.

"We need a house."

He *knew* something had been brewing in her thoughts. The way the gray swirled in those eyes of hers as she munched the raw coconut he'd managed to hack open, the calculated stare off into the distance – it all pointed to one thing. She wanted something.

"I agree. Atlanta, D.C., or Colorado?" He grinned at her, perched on the snaky trunk of a palm.

A smile broke out on her face like the sunset over the Rockies. "Yeah, we'll have to talk about that too. My apartment- that is, *our* apartment - won't work for long."

"Not if we want to start a family."

The rosy blush, the dimple – adorable, even covered in sand and salt and the first stage of sunburn. *God, I don't deserve her. Someone with my roughened edges shouldn't have someone so innocent and fresh.*

She looked away and cleared her throat, still smiling. "Mmm-hmm. But for right *now,* we need something to protect us from the elements."

"Yep. We certainly do. Come on – let's find a place to build it." He took her hand in his. "What'll it be? A hut, a lean-to, or your standard shack?"

"Do they make a deluxe-size shack?" She wrinkled her nose at him and batted her eyelashes.

"Shoulda known you'd want custom!" Even as he joked, he scanned their surroundings, knowing that harm could await them around every turn. In the thick jungle, anything could be hidden.

It took them nearly the rest of the day to gather enough materials – palm leaves, wood, and vine – to begin forming the basic structure for their hut. The location: A raised slope overlooking a blue lagoon, conveniently within yards of a grove of plantain trees they'd found.

"Can't beat this view!" Cara laughed as she gazed out to the ocean.

"I'm with you on that!" He brushed the sweat from his forehead. It was hard work, mentally as well as physically. Every moment, his mind was on alert, scanning and deciding whether they were about to walk into or touch another horrible trap. Their survival didn't just depend on living through the elements and lack of food and fresh water. Cooper had added booby traps as an insult overlaying injury.

Hours later, he and his wife stood back and surveyed their first home, built with their own two hands. It wasn't quite Better Homes and Gardens-worthy, but the roof was sturdy enough and the raised platform of the floor would keep them out of reach of anything crawling along the ground. They even had walls of palm thatch, with an opening for an entrance – and to see the lagoon.

"Looks great, honey." Cara hugged his waist with one arm, still gazing at their roughly fashioned abode.

"Eh, it'll do." His stomach growled. "Time to eat."

He picked several plantains, noticing with dismay that there were less ripe ones than unripe, inedible fruits. They'd need to search for more food soon, and get clever about more ways to gather fresh water.

They could be safe and sheltered, but without fuel and hydration for their bodies, they were toast.

Greg scraped his boots on the mat outside the ranch house and crept inside, silently, as if he were a cat burglar. He had a perfect right to be headed to his room in the basement, but didn't want to be observed.

Every time he entered the house, he felt the sense that he must be on his guard. More than once, he'd turned a corner of a hall to see a strange man or two glaring at him. Or worse, Samir – Cooper's right-hand thug, a huge Egyptian. The man seemed to have eyes – glittery, slanted ones - in every corner of the property.

He reached his room without incident and closed the solid wood door behind him, turning the key in the lock.

Now he'd find out what Cooper had been up to in Sydney.

From a hidden compartment inside the old desk pushed against the wall, he slid out a black box. Opening that, he pulled out the device and earbuds to play back the audio from the bug in Cooper's hat.

The whirring of the helicopter drowned out the first hour of sound. He scrolled past that quickly. Next the smooth silence of the private jet, interrupted only by a few inane remarks on the weather from Cooper's wife and questions from the attendant as to what they'd have to drink.

Greg shifted in his seat – an old chair with a cracked vinyl cushion – rubbed his forehead. All was normal and aboveboard. As the sounds of swelling orchestra music filled the earbuds, he wondered if Cooper truly had just been taking Victoria to the ballet. But then-

"I'll be right back, dahlin'."

Where is he going?

Minutes passed with only background sounds. Then Cooper had a conversation in some kind of tiled, echoey room with a raspy-throated man. Their words raised the hair on the back of Greg's neck. An arms deal of some kind. A delivery date. *Tomorrow!*

Then, payment. Cooper's rare throaty chuckle. "Ah hope that's enough money to last ya a few days."

A sneer, then a door closing.

I knew it! When the hour comes, I'll be ready. No sleep for him tonight. He had too much to plan.

Night fell quickly on the island, the sun all at once dropping below the horizon like a basketball into a hoop, going out in a blaze of orange. He and Cara settled in to their hut for the night, but their minds were too occupied for sleep.

"Hey hon, what's the plan for tomorrow?" In the dimming light coming through the thatch roof, he could see the quiet confidence on her face. She trusted him.

"I don't want to just take Cooper's word for it that this is an island. I'd like to either walk the perimeter or climb those central cliffs to get a better viewpoint."

Cara shifted her position, leaning closer to him. "I like the idea of climbing up to see the island. That'll give us a good view of the whole thing and we can look for promising places to find food." A grin curved one side of her mouth. "Multitasking!"

"An excellent point." He clasped his hands together and tucked them behind his head. "I'd like to try spearfishing in the lagoon tomorrow, and maybe get some fire going so we can roast whatever I catch."

She groaned. "Ohh, that sounds nice."

The hunger gnawed at his own stomach. *Time to change the subject.* "And we can also create some giant letters on the beach for any aircraft passing overhead, or Agency satellites."

Her jaw dropped. "I can't believe I didn't think of that! Will the Agency realize we're missing, or did you tell them not to bother us?"

A sinking feeling hit his core, and it wasn't hunger this time. He *had* told the Agency not to contact him. But he did have to contact *them* every 48 hours, and tonight that would come overdue. Hope stirred. "They'll know I'm in trouble when I miss my check-in." He wrapped his arm around her and held her close. "They'll come for us. Don't worry."

Or will Mark and Angel think I'm playing hooky? Please, God. Alert them to the danger we're facing.

CHAPTER FIVE

The Team Assembles

Agent Angelwing brushed her fingers through her hair and tumbled around the wavy chestnut locks. She blew out an apprehensive sigh. "Honey, will you look at this?"

Across the small office they shared at the Agency, her husband turned around at his desk and rolled his chair to her side in one smooth push. "What is it, love?" He sipped from his mug of morning coffee.

"This." She turned her gaze back to the cold glow of her computer screen, and the image of a photocopied message scrawled on a telegram.

"I WILL HAVE REVENGE FOR JACK'S MURDER. BEWARE THE BLACK SWAN."

She could almost sense the gears clicking in his mind as Agent Markdown processed the threat. His gaze flicked to the list of results of the tests the team had run on the paper and the location it had been discovered – a dead drop they used for snitches. No fingerprints on paper or envelope. Cheap quality paper. Number two pencil lead.

"Have they figured out what the words 'Jack's Murder' are referring to?" He turned his intense gaze on her face.

"This is where it gets interesting." Angel grabbed the printout and held it in front of them. "There are, of course, a lot of matches, but the Crypto department believes it's referencing the death of one John (Jack) Farnsworth. He was shot by one of our agents in a pizza parlor in New Jersey after he fired shots aimed to kill, attempting to protect his boss – Habrin Merkochaz. He fell against sharp metal and sustained a fatal impact to the back of his skull."

Markdown whistled. "Wow." His brow wrinkled. "Hang on a sec. Wasn't that Bryce's first case?"

Angel tapped a few keys, clicked. "Yes!" Her focus raced along the lines of text, skimming for the cream, details that mattered. "Look. Jack's much older brother, Cooper Farnsworth, threatened to sue after Jack died in the hospital." She sat back in her chair. "I remember that! He was furious about the whole situation."

"And the fact that Jack was working as a mercenary in the empire of a murderer and human trafficker – *and* fired first at an international special agent – was merely a blip on his radar." Markdown shook his head, causing his bangs to slip and expose the edge of the scar on his forehead.

She reached up and smoothed his hair back in place. "Do you think this could have any connection to Ryan Black – I mean, "Beware the Black Swan?!" Huh! How about that?"

He found her hand and squeezed it. "I doubt that very much. I know we didn't discover the body, but I saw him fall from that castle wall into the rocks and water below. No mortal could have survived that."

"An associate of his, then?"

"Possibly. Either way, I think we should give Bryce a call, honeymoon or no."

She grinned. "He will *kill* you for interrupting their getaway."

His eyes danced. "Then that's a risk I'll have to take." He leaned over and gave her a quick kiss, then grabbed his cell phone.

She went back to reviewing the alert report, but looked up moments later when she heard him groan.

He was frowning and staring at his phone. "I called his emergency line. He's not answering."

She suppressed her laughter. "I wouldn't worry. They could be-" she coughed – "in their hotel room."

"Well it's stupid of him to ignore his emergency line, even so." He tossed his phone onto the desk. "I'll try him again later."

Agent Angelwing strode back into the Agency's top floor, decked out like your average publishing office. In her hands, two Styrofoam containers, still warm from the toasted deli sandwiches – and all-important pickle spears – inside. *Wish we could have these delivered.* Of course, the secrecy their offices demanded made that impossible, so she or Mark was forced to go get their food if they didn't feel like packing a lunch.

The receptionist's face was drawn tight with worry. "I'm glad you're back. Markdown wants to speak to you right away."

Angel nearly dropped the sandwiches in her haste to traverse through the secret closet elevator and across the 4th underground floor of their base. Finally, she reached their office and pulled open the door.

Markdown turned to face her. Worry lines creased his face as well. "Hey hon. I still can't get ahold of Bryce or Cara. No answer on both of their cell phones and he hasn't called me back. And I've just been informed that he missed his mandatory 48-hour check-in."

She tossed the bag from the deli on the counter, sandwiches forgotten. Her stomach had turned into a ball of knots anyway. "What? Bryce has never skipped a check-in."

"I know. This is more than a pair of elusive honeymooners." He drew a deep breath. "We need to go to the boss."

"Come on." She grabbed for his hand like a drowning person for a life jacket. He was her anchor, she his sail.

They speed-walked to Monty's office and were admitted by a gruff "Come."

Her husband opened the door. "Monty, we have a situation."

Their boss held up a coffee-colored finger. "Hold that thought." He reached for another doughnut from the box on his desk. "I don't know if I can take another situation today." He said as he munched the glazed ring. "Don't even ask how it's going in

81

Moscow with the art forgery scandal, or in Kansas with agent Cobalt and the missing E.M.E.R.A.L.D files." Monty sighed. "All right, hit me with it."

Mark's hand squeezed hers a little tighter before he spoke. "Bryce is MIA."

The doughnut dropped from Monty's hand onto the black surface of his desk. "When did we last hear from him?"

"Too long ago. He missed the 48-hour check, and we need to question him concerning a threat we received connected with his first case and the death of one Jack Farnsworth." Markdown blinked. "He may already be in danger."

Monty looked down, realizing he'd dropped his dessert. Picked up the doughnut. Smushed the whole thing in his mouth, chewed once, gulped down several swallows of coffee. Slammed the mug on the desk. "Anyone but Bryce." He cursed softly. "No offense to you two, but he's my top agent – if we lose him –"

"-We WON'T." Angel felt the words burst from her like a geyser. "What's our next step?"

The fear dissolved in an instant from Monty's face, replaced by grim determination. "Contact his family. I know we try to keep a low profile with agent's loved ones, but we have to know if they've heard from him. But do it discreetly."

She and Mark nodded sharply, as one. "We're on it."

Blake had been excited when Penny accepted his invitation for lunch, and sitting across from her now at the charming Thai restaurant, the smell of chicken masala swirling in the air, things couldn't be better.

Penny's laugh and smile were amazing. And her wit! The girl was clever and hysterically funny. She kept him on his toes throughout their dinner conversation. He was just about to make a smart comeback to her teasing about his love of bright ties when his cell phone buzzed.

He wanted to ignore it, but it could be a client. He apologized to Penny and answered. "Hello, this is Blake Reynolds, can I help you find your dream home?"

A dry cough. "Um, no thanks. I'm calling for a different reason."

A man's voice. Warm, baritone. Oddly familiar, but he couldn't name them. "Who is this?"

"Mark Benson – we were groomsmen together in your brother's wedding just a couple days ago?"

He felt like slapping himself in the face. "Mark! Good to hear from you, man! How's it going?"

"Yeah, not sure – have you heard from Bryce at all? We need his input on something at work." There was something weird underlying Mark's tone. A certain strained vibe.

"The dude's on his honeymoon – of course I haven't heard from him." He laughed, but no answering laugh met his.

"Well… we were hoping you'd been contacted by your brother. Something's come up." The tension had heightened.

"What is it?" Blake demanded. "He's my brother, you can tell me."

A few seconds of silence, then a heavy sigh. "I wish I could tell you about it, Blake. You're a good guy. Unfortunately, I'm not at liberty to-"

He wasn't having any of that government runaround. "-Wait a sec. Don't give me that. Please. What's going on?"

Penny's eyes widened, and her fairy-dust freckles stood out on her suddenly pale face.

Another sigh. At least Mark hadn't hung up. "Bryce has missed a check-in required by the Agency. We're slightly concerned." But there was more than slight concern in his voice. He sounded anxious.

Blake pressed the phone more tightly against his ear. *The Agency? Is Bryce an… Agent?* "What exactly does my brother do for the government, again?"

A short, incredulous laugh. "Gosh, the man is good at keeping secrets."

"What?"

"Oh – nothing. Look, Blake, thank you for your time, and please don't hesitate to contact us at this number if you have any information that could be of use concerning your brother."

"Wait-!"

"Goodbye." He hung up.

Dread coursed through him like a drenching of cold water, erasing the cozy feel the Thai restaurant and Penny's charming company had created. *Bryce is in trouble, and I'm in the dark about it.*

"What was that all about?" Penny's forehead wrinkled in the center.

"Uh – apparently, that was one of Bryce's coworkers. They need to talk to him and haven't been able to get ahold of him."

"Well, duh, he's on his honeymoon! With my best friend!" Penny's frustration sparked in her blue eyes.

"I know... but it was the way the guy acted. He seemed tense, like something was up that he wasn't telling me about. He did mention that Bryce missed some sort of check-in." *Who needs to check in to work on their honeymoon, anyway? Navy SEALs? Or...*

"What does Bryce do for a living? Cara hasn't said so much as a peep, besides that he's a hardworking man and has a steady government job-" Penny's jaw dropped. "Wait a sec... check-in?"

"I know. That sounded off to me too." He looked down at his now-empty plate. "I actually don't know for sure exactly what he does." It stung a little to admit it – that Bryce had never confided in him about his work.

Penny leaned back in her chair. "That's... but only people who are in national security or intelligence can't talk about their jobs, right?" Penny's voice was getting faster and faster, and so was her breathing.

"Well, I think so-"

"My best friend has married someone with a dangerous top-secret job?!?" She interrupted him with an upraised hand. "And now he's "missed a check-in"?!"

Blake looked around. The other diners were starting to take notice and stare. "Penny..."He spoke slowly and softly. "Let's take this outside."

"I-" she halted, pressing her lips in a thin line. "Yeah, okay."

He asked for the check and left a generous tip, then escorted the distressed damsel to his car and opened the passenger door for her. She leaped inside, clutching her purse close. Anxiety still clouded her face.

He hopped into the driver's seat and closed his door, encasing them in their own shell of privacy. "Okay. Look, everything's going to be all right. Bryce is an extremely honorable and responsible man, has been all his life. He will not let Cara be hurt, even if he's in some kind of trouble." He spoke quickly so that she couldn't break in. "I'll call back and ask to speak to his boss."

Penny sighed, looking up towards the roof of the car. "Something is very wrong, Blake. I can sense it. They're in danger."

"Let's not jump to conclusions yet." Blake dialed the number Mark had given him. "In the meantime, why don't you call her mom and see if she's heard from Cara?"

Penny whipped out her phone. "You got it."

As she waited for someone to pick up, he heard Mark come on the line on his own phone. "This is Agent Markdown."

AGENT MARKDOWN? What in the world? "Mark?"

"Oh, hello Blake. What information do you have for me?"

"First I need some from you! Or actually, from your boss. I have to speak to Mr. Montrose – or does he have a code name I should be using?!" Blake could hear the ire in his voice, plus it was burning in his gut. *I gotta calm down, or they won't take me seriously.*

"Ah, well... all right. Hold please."

Penny had started speaking into her phone, holding a hand over the ear closest to him. "Miz Naomi? Oh, it's good to hear your voice. Have you heard from Cara yet?" He had to commend her on how calm she was keeping her tone.

"Montrose."

He turned his attention back his conversation. "Yes, this is Blake Reynolds, and I need to know what's going on with my brother. Has he disappeared?"

A few seconds of silence. "Mr. Reynolds, you sound just like your brother over the phone. Pity it isn't him I'm speaking to, as we'd very much like to consult him about something at the moment."

"About *what?*"

Muffled voices in the background. Then, "I'm afraid I can't tell you what about, but I can tell you that your brother was supposed to check in with this office every 48 hours in case of emergency. He has already missed that by over 12 hours, which has caused great concern. Now a situation has arisen, but we cannot contact him. So please, if you come up with any information, share it with us immediately."

"Wha-" the line went dead before he could speak again. "Mmmh!" He grunted in frustration.

Penny was just finishing her conversation with Cara's mother. "Thank you. I will. Take care." She hung up. Looked at him. "She hasn't heard from her. And come to think of it, there's been nothing on her Facebook or Instagram feeds, either."

Blake gripped the steering wheel with an iron fist, then started the motor with a harsh twist of the key. "All right, that's it. I am going to fly out to that Turtle Bay place and deal with this myself. No sitting on my hands for me!"

He didn't even get the car out of the parking lot before Penny shouted. "I'm coming with you!"

Girl, you are nuts. Penny threw another shirt into her carry-on. *First paying for a bridesmaids' dress, now adding a plane ticket to Hawaii to the bill for this month?*

Good thing she was just starting to collect royalties on the *Wrinkles the Baby Elephant* storybook.

Her cell phone jingled. "Hello?"

Blake's friendly tone flowed into her ears. "Hey, it's me. I've got our tickets. Our flight leaves at six o'clock."

"Tonight?!"

"No, tomorrow morning."

"Oh, right. Ugh. Okay – how much do I owe you?"

"Nothing!" he insisted, "I'm the one who came up with this crazy plan, you just play sidekick and all expenses will be paid."

Warmth flooded her heart. *What a sweet guy.* "Blake, I can't let you do that..."

"Why not? You're not a flaming feminist, you've let me open doors for you-"

"Well, you don't have to be my sugar daddy and pay for my expensive plane fare."

He laughed, heartily, a beautiful sound. "Let's call an end to the war of the stereotypes, please. You can make it up to me later."

A little nervous tingle went through her. "How?"

"Another date, once we get back from the tropics." He paused. "Or while we're there."

It was hardly a struggle to accept his terms. "Sure."

After speaking to the resort manager, who had been unable to give him any information about Bryce and Cara Reynolds, Benjamin Montrose threw up his hands. "That's it! I've had it!" He looked at agent Markdown. "Select eight other agents who have had search and rescue experience and meet me in the maroon conference room."

"Yes, sir!"

"We are going to get them back, whatever it takes." *I will not lose Bryce. He's like the son I never had.*

Moments later, eleven people sat at the long black table in the maroon conference room. The room itself was not maroon, it was named after special Agent Maroon, who had given his life in a high-risk mission and stabilized the safety of the nation of Morocco in the process.

Montrose stared thoughtfully at the ten agents before him. Markdown and Angelwing, the dedicated husband-wife duo. Mark had selected eight others whose impressive track records and skills spoke for themselves – agents Pearlwind, Bluebeard, Northstar, Spartan, Goldenrod, Wildcat, Darknight, and... Toadspeckle. The last member of the team, a pasty-faced number-cruncher, rather threw him, but when he remembered that Todd (or Toady, as he was nicknamed) was one of their top data analysts, he nodded approval.

Mark stood and gave a quick rundown of the mission, outlining the plan and possible dangers involved. This was the moment for any of the agents to turn down the chance to be involved. But being specially selected for a task to recover one of their own was an honor, and they knew it. Every agent responded in the affirmative with fire in their eyes – all but Toadspeckle, who agreed with mild interest.

At last, satisfied, Montrose sent them off to board the incredibly fast private plane that would take them to their destination in nearly a quarter of the time of a standard trip to Hawaii.

"Good luck, Mark." He clapped his hand on Markdown's shoulder as he led his team from the room.

A brisk nod was the only response. Agent Markdown had gone into action mode.

Once the group had left, one solitary man entered after them. Shadowchaser nodded a greeting, caution etched on his face and wariness in his nearly-black eyes. The guy never relaxed, even in the Agency headquarters.

"Trent, thanks for coming. I've got something important for you." Montrose didn't bother asking the man to sit, knowing he'd rather stay standing on guard.

"Yes, Sir. I'm ready." He owned a smooth, quiet voice. Perfect for the task ahead.

"I can see that. I'm assigning you to protect Bryce's family while we deal with this revenge threat. I've already talked to them. I want somebody guarding his mother and sister in case they become the next target, and I believe you're the man for the job."

Trent straightened his muscled shoulders. "Thank you, Sir. I'm grateful for the chance to help Bryce in any way."

Monty grunted. "Saved your life too, has he?"

"Yes, Sir."

"Seems to be a habit of his."

A hot, sultry afternoon out on the island found Bryce and Cara hiking "Mount Perception" as they'd named it, since it would allow them to perceive the situation and see everything below it. Since they had no shoes, Bryce had wrapped several thick layers of tough palm leaf around their respective feet and tied it with twine.

Two-thirds up the steep slope now, they could see much of what they needed to. This side of the island had the stretch of beach where they'd landed, the clearing where they'd gathered water and almost been sliced to bits, and the circular lagoon of blue water near their hut, and the plantain trees. Intermingling all that was thick, bushy jungle vegetation.

"How long till we reach the summit?" Cara asked him, valiantly striding along.

He tugged at her arm. "Not so fast. We shouldn't be overexerting ourselves."

She slowed. "You're right."

"Don't worry. We'll reach the top soon. Think about something else."

"Hmm." She tapped her chin with one finger. The princess-cut diamond on her ring flashed spangles of aquamarine-hued light. She smiled as it caught her eye. "I love my ring!"

He smiled. "I'm delighted that you like it." Picking it out had been more of a challenge than most of his top-secret missions combined.

"It's exactly the shade of Caribbean water." Then she moaned. "Now I'm thirsty again. Sorry. You never realize how much water you need to drink until you only have a few drops a day."

"Now's probably a good time to stop and drink these." Bryce held up the small coconuts that were tied at his waist.

They refreshed themselves with the coconut water and sat in the shade for a few minutes. Insects hummed in the trees and birds called from afar. Even the silence held sounds.

And then a sound that was most definitely out of place.

"Mmmmhhrrrrr. Mmmmmmhhrr." Horrified, he and Cara stared at each other.

No way. Couldn't be. Their minds must be playing tricks on them.

Again, the deep, rumbling roars echoed from what sounded like miles away.

"Lions?!" Cara's voice rasped with terror. "What in the world?!"

"Why would there be lions on this island? This is not their natural habitat. Unless Cooper..." He trailed off, not wanting to voice the thought in his mind. But his wife finished it for him.

"Unless Cooper put them here, like those swinging blades!"

He took her hand and rubbed the back of it with his thumb. "Hey. We'll be all right. Big cats are more scared of you than you are of them." Besides, he had a machete strapped to his leg. Armed thusly, he could handle up to twenty ninja monks – and knew this from experience.

"Come on." He stood. "Let's reach the top of that mountain."

She followed him, still clinging to his hand.

At last, on top of the mountain, they had a 360-degree view of the island on which they stood. It was definitely an island. Blue water stretched to the edge of the horizon all the way around. On the half of the island they hadn't explored yet, cliffs fell to the ocean on one side, then sloped to a beach on the other half studded with tide pools and seaweed-strewn rocks. And from the mountain to the water's edge stretched the thickest of tropical foliage.

Anything could be lurking in that.

"Mmmmhhhrrrrr. Mmmhhhrr."

They spent the day without food and with plenty of frights — namely lion roars, also snare-traps made with ropes and bent trees, and patches of muck that she insisted was quicksand, but Bryce wasn't convinced after he tossed a branch in and it floated.

Desperately hungry, they gulped down some raw birds' eggs they'd taken from ledges on Mount Perception. Tomorrow, Bryce promised, they'd look for a cave to barricade themselves in case of lion attacks, and also start a fire so they could cook some of their food. He was hopeful of finding some shellfish in the tide pools, or spearing something in the lagoon.

Just before night fell, a cloudburst gathered overhead and dropped down rain. They leaped around gathering rainfall in leaves, coconut shells, anything that would hold water – and drank as much as they could straight from the sky.

Oh Lord, she silently prayed, snuggled close to Bryce's side in their hut that night, *Please keep watching over us. Please send rescue, someone to find us. And please, please, keep us safe from harm and danger.*

CHAPTER SIX

Sabotage and Seafood

Under the cover of the darkness spread across the Australian sky, the Black Swan glided closer and closer to her new port – but it wouldn't be home for long. The submarine would only be docked in the underground bay for a few short days, and then the power of her nuclear ship-launched missile would be unleashed and aimed at the fault line running underneath California's golden coast. Striking at the precise point would cause the whole state to crumble into the ocean.

Forget two measly twin buildings. Cooper knew gloating was bad luck, but at this point, didn't care. *My strike on that pompous, overfed, crass nation will be a thousand times more deadly and shocking.*

One highly prized and overlooked feature of his property was the fact that along the north border, it connected to the coast. The discovery of the watery grotto embedded in one spot like a cavity in a tooth had sparked the whole idea of owning a secret boat. One whose bite would be infinitely worse than her silent bark.

Now he waited, with trusted Samir at his side and a handful of men, in the dark grotto lit only by LED lanterns, for his prize to arrive.

At last, contact with the deliverymen via his mobile phone. They were here, waiting for his invitation to enter the mouth of the grotto. He gave the signal, speaking into the radio. "Waltz on in, Matilda."

Slowly, agonizingly slowly to him, the sub moved into place, surfaced like a little whale, water rushing off the sides, glimmering in the near-blackness.

He felt almost paternal, as if watching his baby be born. She would make him proud on her crowning day of victory.

Dread clutched in Greg's gut from where he watched, tucked in a crevice of the grotto, as the sub arrived in all her menacing glory. Hidden deep in her belly, the Tomahawk nuclear missile, able to launch from the submarine *while it was underwater*, and travel thousands of miles to its predetermined target in a matter of minutes. Or at least, that's what the terrorist had promised Cooper on the audio.

He shifted, one of his legs cramping up. *Dang. Not as young as I used to be.* In the good ol' days when he was a strapping young intelligence agent, a little stakeout work was a piece of cake. Now his hair had grayed, his eyes were framed in lines, and his aging body made him aware every day of what he'd lost.

Dawn's beautiful face floated before him, obscuring the sight of the men working to secure the sub to its moorings. The smiles of his three adorable children – Bryce, Blake, and Bethany, haunted him.

How he'd ever had the strength to leave them, to do what was right for their safety, and not tell them why... he would never know. Maybe God had been helping him, although at the time it seemed he'd never been farther away.

Footsteps crunched, coming closer, and he crouched low and ducked behind the rocky outcropping. Steeled his nerves for the moment he was discovered. But the man walked past, headed in the direction that would eventually take him to the ranch house.

He risked a glance. Definitely Samir, from the proud stance and the way he swaggered slightly when he walked. The man always looked like he was gazing upon the amazing pyramids of his ancestors – and could probably trace his family tree all the way back to the pharaohs.

Greg breathed a silent sigh of relief. *If he'd seen me – this would all be over.* Samir was the type to kill first and ask questions later – or not to bother with the questions at all, as he dropped the dead body at the foot of his master like a cat with a prized dead chipmunk.

It was time to get out of there and report to his contact. Too much had happened to conceal it any longer.

The question is... will they believe me? His story would sound pretty far-fetched. *Maybe I should sleep on it and gather my thoughts together.* It would not do to sound incoherent when speaking to the one man who still believed in him.

Penny braced herself as the tram whooshed through the underground tunnel, headed to Gate B. The Atlanta airport was packed with people, even busier than the last time she'd been here, when she and Naomi and Nana had picked Cara and Bryce up after their trip to Europe. Penny felt safer with Blake at her side. He formed a comforting buffer between her and the other people riding the airport tram. She hooked her elbow around the metal pole and hung on tight as the tram's automated voice asked that all passengers please prepare to stop. The doors opened.

"All passengers for Gate B may now depart."

"That's us!" Blake grinned and rolled out their luggage – two carry-ons as large as the maximum limit would allow.

The airline also allowed one "Personal" item. So, over her shoulder hung her signature purse – a gigantic peach leather number that she adored for its abilities to hold whatever she needed.

"Coming!" Penny followed Blake's long, smooth stride as they exited the tram and started down the huge, wide hallway, brightly lit from all angles.

They separated at the men's and women's restrooms, indicated with big pink and blue figures shining above the entrances, and after that quick stop, ordered breakfast from the Chick-fil-a and checked in at their gate.

"Man, nine hours? It wasn't that long from Colorado."

She laughed. "Um, not surprising, considering that's practically all the way across the country."

"True." He unwrapped his chicken biscuit and dug in.

Penny spooned a mouthful of her fruit-and-yogurt parfait. Last time, she and Cara had spent the whole trip whispering in each other's ear and laughing. She tried to keep the worry and dread at bay, chewing and swallowing quickly.

"So, you've met my family, tell me about yours." Blake sipped his coffee.

Oh boy. Forget can of worms. Her family was a barrel of snakes. "Do we *have* to talk about them? There's not much to tell."

His eyebrow quirked in suspicion. "Maybe not, but I'd still like to hear about them. They can't be *that* bad." He flashed a grin as wide as a melon slice.

You... have... no... idea. "Uh, okay. Well – my parents raised us as hippie flower children. We grew up homeschooled and eating whole grains and bean sprouts. My older sister Lindy terrorized me with her freakish Pekinese, which I hated, and my younger sister recently ran away and married a shoe salesman and I haven't seen her since. Also, I haven't spoken to my parents since their divorce."

"Wow." Sympathy colored Blake's voice. "What's your younger sister's name?"

Penny selected a strawberry with her spoon before answering. "Bluebell."

Blake started to laugh, then gulped. "Uhhh…"

She laughed. "It's okay. I know — it's a ridiculous name. Are you deducing anything about my parents from that?"

He smiled. "They must be interesting characters."

"Yep. They are. So I pretty much did my own thing in my teen years, but thankfully I had Cara and her very stable mom and Grandma, as a second family."

"Aw, that's great. They're precious people." Blake polished off his biscuit with two last bites.

"Passengers for flight 109, Atlanta to Hawaii, may now begin boarding."

"Aha!" Blake tossed his wrapper in the trash and reached for her hand. "Time to begin our adventure. Let's go find Bryce and Cara."

Once on board the plane, Penny felt her nerves begin to tingle. *I wonder how Mason felt on that tinier plane.* The stewardesses bustled around preparing for liftoff, and she and Blake found their seats and stowed their luggage.

Penny looked out the window at the tarmac and the little people down below wearing neon safety vests, doing their work on the ground to make sure the planes entered and exited the hangars safely.

His friend promised he would fly him safely to his grandma's funeral. Ohio. Such a long way away... Still, closer than Hawaii.

Blake buckled his seatbelt and tested the seat's reclining back. "Not bad."

She murmured incoherently in response. Being with Blake, instead of laughing and talking with Cara on the last plane ride, was stirring memories. *I didn't want him to go. But he was determined. The pet store owner gave him the time off, he had a free ride, and his grandma was like another mother to him.* Sorrow washed over her again in chilling waves.

And then the phone call. Mason's cell. She'd answered, full of joy, ready to talk to her beloved. The only guy she'd ever loved.

"Hey hottie! How's it going?"

"Penny. I love you." His voice – ragged, raw. Full of pain.

"Mason, what's wrong?" Dread filling her soul, she waited several agonizing seconds for his response.

"Our plane's gone down. We crashed in some treetops." He rasped. "Called the authorities. On their way." He took a heaving breath. "But darling, I don't think I'm gonna make it. I want to, so bad. But I feel it. I'm fading."

Desperation clawing at her throat in a stranglehold, she choked out her words. "No! Oh baby – I love you! You have to hang in there!" An ocean of tears splashed down her cheeks.

"I'm so sorry I can't kiss you goodbye." He wheezed, his tenor voice a mere echo of the usual warm sound.

"No, no! Don't go! Don't go! I need you. Please." She pleaded, sobbing now, crumpling down on her kitchen floor, hair spilling across the tile.

"I'm sorry." A raspy sob. "I love you, baby girl. I always will." The words were coming with great effort now, slower. "See you on the other side."

"Penny? Are you okay? You're crying." Blake touched her arm, concern radiating in his voice.

Of course she was crying. She'd cried so hard after Mason's voice had gone and the line went dead that she'd lost her voice and her face had puffed up like a pink marshmallow.

She swiped roughly at her face now, not daring to look at Blake. She kept her nose pointed out the window. "Y-yup. Sorry." Emotion quavered in her voice.

"No, it's okay, I was just wondering what the matter was."

At that moment, the plane reversed, then started heading down the runway. The attendants demonstrated emergency protocol, the copilot's voice calmly rumbling over the sound of the engines, asking them to fasten their seatbelts and make sure the seats were in the upright position.

"Um… nothing." She couldn't explain. No one had known about Mason. Fear of her parents' reactions to knowing she was dating a college dropout working a minimum-wage job had pressured them into keeping their relationship a secret.

"Okay."

But then the plane began galloping down the runway, nose tilted to the heavens. Penny's heart pounded, her ears hurt, her throat was closing in sheer terror. She gasped, hyperventilating.

"Penny?!" Blake grasped her hand in his and she gripped it like a lifeline.

I don't want to die. The thought absolutely shocked her. Fear injected into her veins at the sheer speed they were hurtling through space on their journey into the sky. Fear of death.

For the first time since the death of her fiancé, she realized she *didn't* want to die and be with him. *I want to live!* She hadn't even fully known that she'd hungered for death, hoped this life would just magically quit so she didn't have to go on without him.

The horror and relief created a strange blend of feelings exploding in her chest. Her breathing slowed to normal, and she took an extra-deep breath, filling her lungs to max capacity with oxygen.

"Sir, is she all right?" One of the flight attendants inquired of Blake.

"I'm not sure."

Penny finally turned her head to look at the flight attendant. "Yes. Thank you." They nodded, walked off. She turned her gaze to Blake's gorgeous brown eyes.

"I have a lot to tell you." She squeezed his hand, still holding hers.

His face, a mixture of bewilderment and worry, smoothed. "I thought so." His eyebrows rose. "But honestly, are you okay? Do you need anything? Glass of water?"

"I'll be all right. But I will take some ice water when they bring the drinks cart around." She sighed, releasing it all.

"Sounds good." He waited.

"So. The freakout episode that just happened." She gulped back the tears in her throat. "I knew this guy... this wonderful, sweet guy..." A few more drops trickled down her cheek, and she patted them away. "He died in a plane crash."

Amazement, horror, sympathy, all played across Blake's features. "Oh. *Man.* That's rough."

"You don't know the half of it." She shook her head. "Cara doesn't even know about this. No one does."

His eyes grew bigger. "Why don't they know, Penny?"

"It's... it's complicated. *Really* complicated." She coughed. "Remember my sister, Bluebell? After she ran away with Ricardo the smooth-talking shoe salesman, our parents flipped their lids. Forbade my older sister and me to date or marry anyone less than a doctor, lawyer, or millionaire."

Blake nodded encouragement to keep going.

"Well, Mason's fortune was next to nothing. He was just your average guy, with a minimum wage job at a pet store."

"A pet store." Blake smiled. "I like this guy already."

She found herself smiling in return. "He loved animals. Tulip, my canary, was a gift from him."

"Ahh." Understanding dawned on his face. "This explains so much."

"Yep. I have a good reason for being an emotional maniac."

He laughed, dimples creasing his cheeks. "Not in the least."

"You're too generous." She brushed her hair away from her face. "But anyway... He asked me to marry him. I said yes. But then his grandma passed away. He was flying up to the funeral in Ohio with a friend of his in a tiny little plane, and they had some kind of altimeter malfunction and ran into a heavy fog, and..." The lump came back. "...They crashed into a forest. The plane was destroyed. They said it was a miracle the two men lived long enough to call for help."

Blake raised the arm rest between them until it was vertical and out of the way, then settled his arm around her shoulders. The wordless comfort he offered meant more than anything he could have said.

That'd been her fear, that if she told anyone, they would either say she should be brave and get over it, or they would murmur tired platitudes that only made her feel awful.

She rested her head against Blake's warm shoulder. "Thanks."

"What do you *mean*, there's no sign of them anywhere?" Angelwing demanded, pounding her palm against the resort manager's desk. "Are you telling me they've vanished into thin air?"

The mild-mannered Hawaiian shrugged, his half-moon eyes widened in fear. "I'm sorry, lady, but the couple have not been spotted anywhere since they left the dining room on Tuesday evening. One of our staff members says she saw them walking towards the beach, but we do not know which direction they went."

"Get that staff member in here. NOW." Angel heard the primal growl underlying her voice, but couldn't hold it back. Not until Bryce and Cara were standing in front of her in perfect safety.

Her husband touched her shoulder and cleared his throat, a silent plea for her to calm down a little. All right. She'd go from a level ten to a level nine. Anything less wouldn't gel with the Mama-bear protection instinct that had kicked in when she heard Bryce was in trouble.

"Yes, yes ma'am. We will bring her here." The man hustled from the room and returned shortly with a wizened older woman. "This is her."

After questioning the lady about the last known Bryce-and-Cara sighting, Angelwing and Markdown split up their team in half and sent them down the beach in either direction from the resort. Three hours later, the team that had headed north reported they'd found something.

She and her husband hurried to the spot on the beach, where Darknight showed them the signs of a struggle he'd discovered in the sand and in the underbrush along the shore. Footprints showed where many men had crouched for some time, hiding in the jungle.

"Who are these men? Man-eating natives?" Pearlwind's creamy skin paled even further.

"Here." Spartan held up a bullet casing, pinched between beefy finger and thumb. "They weren't wild jungle men. They had AK-47's."

Markdown blew out a long breath. "Time to look at some satellite footage."

"Guys!" Goldenrod ran up, curls bouncing. "Look at these!" Hanging from a stick in her hand, two beaded sandals dangled.

"Good job. We'll dust these for fingerprints. Pity we don't have Cara's toe-prints on file." Angel dropped the shoes in a clear evidence bag and clutched it tightly.

"All right everyone, tape this area off and call in the forensics squad." Mark commanded. "Angel and I are headed back to base." He took her hand and they turned and marched towards the resort.

"Don't worry, hun. We'll find them." Mark's voice rumbled low in his chest.

"We'd better, because wherever they are, they're counting on us." *And I will* not *let them down.*

The gnawing hunger, never quite satisfied from chewing coconut meat, had become a constant feeling in his stomach. He knew Cara had to be starving too, even with her lighter calorie needs. They had to get some nourishment in them.

"To the tide pools!" He announced at midday.

His wife, sitting on the ground, looked up at him with a longsuffering expression. "Not sure I'm up for a hike today, sweetheart."

He reached for her hands and helped her to her feet. "I know. But I'm pretty sure those tide pools will have shellfish aplenty. We'll get there somehow, even if I have to carry you across the island."

She shook her head. "No, you can't do that! You'd use up too much energy." He didn't like how her voice sounded weak. It didn't match the determined light in her eye.

"Trust me... we'll make it." *She has no idea of some of the hard things I've done.* But would telling her be encouraging, or scare her? Best hold his silence for now.

They set off along the shore at a leisurely pace. Cutting across the island was the shorter way, but much harder to traverse. It was worth the longer walk to have each step be easier.

At last they had reached the tide pools. Cara rested on a smooth rock to regain some energy while he explored nooks and crannies.

Among the seaweed-crusted rocks, he found crabs, mussels, limpets, and a few starfish. The starfish he left, not sure if it was the edible species or toxic, and unwilling to take the chance at this point.

"Here we go!" He deposited the pile of goodies in front of his wife.

She eyed them, not looking exactly thrilled. "We *are* going to cook these somehow, right? I mean, these little guys are still alive!" One of the crabs waved its claw in the air, as if to prove her point.

"Watch and learn, my princess."

Cara waited patiently while her husband busied himself with the task of starting a fire. *I hope he can do it!* She had faith in his abilities, but didn't see how they could possibly achieve flame with no matches and no lighters whatsoever.

"The key is preparation. Wait here." Bryce walked into the jungle and disappeared for a few minutes. When he came back, he held a pile of materials in his arms. Using some fluffy dried grass and bits of twisted tree bark, he formed a ball about the size of a baseball and set it aside.

"Okay. Let's set the stage." He dug a smooth, shallow pit in the dirt between the sand and the foliage and surrounded it with rocks. Inside the rocks he stacked large and small pieces of dry wood and sprinkled kindling – twigs and small sticks – all through it.

He looked at her and grinned, cheek dimpling in the way she found most irresistible. "Now for the part that takes some finesse."

Bryce took the swiss army knife from his pocket and from another pocket, a small, flat rock.

"Is that flint?" *Maybe this will work!*

"Couldn't find any. It's quartzite, but it should work just as well." He pressed his lips together in concentration and struck the rock and the back of his knife blade together in a quick motion, three times.

On the third try, sparks flew and landed in the middle of the soft nest he'd made with the dry grass and bark. "Yes!" He quickly cupped it in his hands and blew gently until it burst into flame.

"Aaah! You did it!" She couldn't contain her excitement as he dropped the flaming bundle into the center of the kindling and wood. They gradually caught and burned until a small, crackling blaze glowed before their eyes.

"All right! Keep an eye on this and add more kindling if it starts to die out." As she crouched beside their little fire, he raced over to the pile of sea creatures and scooped them up in his hands. He brought them to the fire and carefully laid the mussels and limpets out on the rocks surrounding it. The crabs were stuck on a sharpened stick and held directly above the hot flames to roast.

"Now we wait." Bryce carefully turned the stick holding the crabs so they cooked evenly.

 In almost no time, the heat from the fire cooked the mussels and crabs. The mussel shells opened and the crabs began to steam. He laid everything out on a huge green banana leaf like a seafood platter.

"Okay, *now* I'm impressed!" Cara threw her arms around his torso and kissed him on the lips.

"You're welcome." He murmured when they broke apart. "If that's the thanks I get every time I cook for us, call me Chef Bryce."

She laughed. "Come on, let's eat! I'm famished!" Cara cracked apart a mussel shell and downed the orangey meat in one swallow. She wrinkled her nose and grinned. "Eh, not bad. It could use a little salt."

An idea struck him. "Wait here." He left her sitting cross-legged on the sand near the fire and bounded over to where he'd seen dry salt deposits on the rocks. Using his knife, he scraped some onto a shell. He presented it to his wife as if it were fine china.

"My hero!" She sprinkled a pinch on her next shellfish and declared it much improved from the first one.

"If we're still hungry after this, there's seaweed for dessert. I recognized some of it out there."

Cara squished up her mouth in distaste, laughing. "I think I'm good with this stuff, thanks." She reached for a crab.

After consuming the whole pile of steamed, roasted food, they rested for a few minutes, and then took the opportunity to lay out the word "HELP" high on the beach in huge letters shaped by rocks and branches from the jungle.

Bryce brushed the sand from his hands and looked over their work. "That should do it." He piled some live coals inside a gigantic hollowed-out coconut shell and they set off to return to their hut.

Finally, things were going their way. For now.

They'd finally landed at 3:00 PM, tired and stiff. After her startling confession, Penny slept for most of the plane ride.

He couldn't sleep after that if his life depended on it. His thoughts swam with questions and his heart ached for the pain Penny must be in, to have lost someone she cared about so much.

Maybe... this is why I came. She needs someone to listen.

A short taxi ride, and they were at the resort. Checking in at the front desk in the beautiful lobby was simple enough, plus he scored them adjoining rooms. The cost of the airfare and their rooms was eating into his checking account, but thankfully he'd earned a nice sum from his last house sale and could float on that for a while.

The mood in the lobby was off, somehow. The manager was nowhere to be found and the rest of the staff looked tense and agitated. On one wall, a large poster stated that anyone with any information about Bryce and Cara Reynolds should call the phone number provided, and a picture of the couple was pasted in the center.

After they dropped off their luggage in their absolutely gorgeous rooms, Penny suggested that they walk around the resort and snoop. It sounded good to him, so they took the elevator down to the ground floor.

It was when they reentered the lobby that things got interesting. Marching in, all the way across the brightly-lit space, were Mark and Angel Benson, Bryce's friends – and coworkers. Behind them, a line of people he didn't recognize. Angel immediately spotted him and Penny and her eyes lit with what looked like rage. "You!" She jabbed a finger in their direction.

"In the office! NOW." She did an about-face and walked towards a door, opened it, and waited, glaring at them.

They meekly walked to the office. He was just about to enter the room when Penny squealed.

"Those shoes!" Penny grabbed a pair of sandals in a clear plastic evidence bag right out of Angel's grip. "These are Cara's!"

In an instant, Angel's expression softened. She gently took the bag from Penny and said "Thank you for identifying these. Now please, inside."

They ambled in and sat in the chairs printed with tropical palm leaves, which looked right at home in the island-themed room.

As the door closed behind him with a click, Agent Markdown eyed them. "Now, what are you doing here?"

Blake crossed his arms. "Look. I know you have jobs to do, whatever they are, but if you expect me to just sit back and wait while my brother is miss-"

"Shh." Angel held up a finger. "No need to get testy. The last thing I'd say would be "please remain calm", because obviously your brother's disappearance has greatly upset us all, but we have to stay focused and work together if we want to find them."

The words cooled the fire in his chest. "Work together, ma'am?"

Mark looked less than pleased at the way the conversation was going. "I don't think-"

Angel changed the finger to a whole hand held up like a traffic guard. "Yes, of course we're working together. For one thing, they just came all this way. For another, they've not been here ten minutes and already they've proven to be useful." She nodded to Penny, who was on the edge of her seat.

Penny settled back in the chair, smiling gratefully. "We just want to help. I know ya'll are the professionals and that's just fine, but if we can do *anything*…"

With all three of them staring at him, Markdown sighed and rubbed the back of his head. "Very well." Then he stared at his wife with a firm set to his mouth. "But you owe me one."

She smiled and wrinkled her nose at him. "Okay, babe. I owe you one."

Mark's eyes twinkled with amusement, but then his gaze zeroed onto Blake's face like a sniper's laser. "But there are ground rules."

"Yes!" Angel chimed in.

"Firstly, don't even speak one word to anyone without permission from us. Don't make a move without checking first. We are not your babysitters and you will be expected to patiently wait in the background." With every sentence, Markdown made a hammering motion with pointer finger raised.

"Yeah. We call the shots, kiddos." Angel folded her arms across her chest.

Penny nodded obediently, leaning forward in her seat.

He wasn't sure about being called a kiddo, especially by a woman who had to be only a year or two older than him, but was resolved to do whatever it took if it helped out his brother. "I'm in."

But what am I getting myself into? Now that he was actually in Hawaii, he wasn't sure what he was supposed to do for Bryce.

Uhh… Please, God. Show me. Or I'll look like a buffoon.

"Supply Run" was Greg's excuse. Driving an hour away from the station for a grocery run was considered an easy jaunt in these parts. While in the tiny town, Greg could pick up the week's food supplies for the cook – and get connected to some high-speed internet so he could get a message to his contact.

Oh, Cooper had high-speed internet out at the ranch house, of course, but the last thing Greg wanted was to get caught blabbing by the man he was deliberately betraying. He'd caught some chatter from Cooper's goons about a couple that Cooper had abducted and left on his private island – filling him with even more disgust for his unworthy employer. And now he had the added problem of how to help the poor people who had incurred Cooper's wrath.

He wasted no time loading the crates of fresh produce, flour, milk, and other goods into the stalwart pickup truck, and then parked outside the one bar – which also boasted wi-fi.

He slunk in, nodded to the proprietor, avoided eye contact with the dudes on the barstools, and slumped down in the corner and pulled out his phone.

Eventually, he accessed the right secure online chat room and sent his greeting.

Within minutes, the reply came. His contact was there.

The flower shop is open. He typed. That meant he wanted a meeting. *The Amaryllis bulbs are in stock* – too much to say online. *It's a special order* – extremely urgent.

The reply appeared in a blink. *Do you have Hyacinth?* – Is backup needed? *I'll come for a visit* – Message received. We'll meet. *What time?*

No Hyacinth yet. Tomorrow would be best, if not sooner.

I think I'll buy some roses. Midnight. Same place as last time.

Sounds great.

He signed off, bought a can of Bundaberg ginger beer from the soda machine, and drove back to the station in the midafternoon heat. He'd need to check on the cattle when he arrived, but after that he could review the audio on Cooper's hat bug, and see if he'd said anything of import last evening.

But to his dismay, when he sat in front of his laptop and plugged in the earbuds, there was some audio background noise and then – static. The bug had shorted out.

No more easy route. He'd have to eavesdrop live if he wanted to learn anything.

Blast! It's second-rate, outdated equipment. This would have never happened to him in his days at the Agency. He'd always used top-of-the-line, best-quality supplies for his work.

He could feel the blood pressure rising, pounding in his chest. The anger and hurt of the betrayal, the sudden attack from someone he'd counted on – the fury exploded through him again at the remembrance.

But what hurt the worst was having to abandon his wife and children for their own good. He'd missed so many birthdays, anniversaries, special days... so many 'firsts' in their lives.

All because of a rotten blackmailer.

NO MORE! Greg would have yelled, if it were safe to do so. No. He'd channel this energy into an offensive strike. Then at least when he met with his contact, there would be some good news to share along with the horrific report.

He opened his door and looked both ways down the hall. The coast was clear. He sauntered out and casually closed it and locked it behind himself, tucked his hands in his pockets, and left the ranch house via the back door. Crossed the veranda.

Passed the exotic display of landscaping at the corner of the house.

He saddled up his horse and pointed his nose to the north. If anyone asked, he was surveying the property, checking the foliage to see if the herd could graze here anytime soon. He would have driven a truck, but preferred to go in silence but for the hoofbeats. Didn't want anyone overhearing the motor.

After a long ride, he reached the coast and the north border of the station. The underground grotto lay before him, completely invisible from above. He tied the horse to a eucalyptus tree and sneaked forward on foot. The other night, he'd taken an observation as to where the guards were posted on the submarine, carefully avoiding one of them aboveground, who was taking a smoke. There was one more in the actual grotto.

He entered the hole in the ground and crept along the tunnel, which widened as he got lower. He looked around the rock outcropping into the underground bay. The water glimmered, light from a few holes bringing scant sunlight into the shadowy place.

The guard on duty checked his watch, then set off to stroll around the huge cave.

With a silent, catlike tread, Greg made a series of leaps from shadow to shadow, finally drawing near enough to slip aboard the sub.

The door closed behind him with a quiet clank. He grimaced. Now he'd have to keep one ear attuned to the sound of any approaching guards who may have heard the slight noise.

No time to lose.

The submarine control room was deserted, but still glowed with robotic life. Lights glinted like constellations on a black surface, only laid out in gridlike pattern instead of random splashes of starlight. Dials and levers and knobs jostled for position among the computer display screens.

Greg crouched in front of the main computer hub, slipping on his electromagnetic-sensitive gloves so he could touch the screen without leaving damning fingerprints behind.

Soft "meep-meep-meep" sounds responded to the taps of his gloved fingertips on the screen as he typed a series of commands. His brain, which he'd thought rusty from lack of use, proved it was just as capable as ever as he created a program that would sabotage the system in a way that they could never trace back to this specific time of day and location. *And* would cripple the launch function of the nuclear Tomahawk missile.

There. See how that feels, you stupid dart. Mentally insulting the missile helped him stay loose as he finished his job, though chill sweat dripped down his backbone and a small part of his brain was on the alert should he be interrupted at any second.

But no. Task complete, he stepped away from the computer, wiping his clammy forehead with the back of his hand.

That should do it. I hope.

He left the control room, crept towards the hatch, but then the murmur of approaching voices sent shockwaves down his spine.

CHAPTER SEVEN

Tea and Gingerbread

Hunger partially satiated by the shellfish meal, Cara and Bryce hoarded the coals in the coconut 'bowl' until they were at the hut by the secluded lagoon once more. It was now late in the afternoon.

Cara watched as her husband banked a fire to maintain their precious source of cooking heat. "I find it amazing that my husband is such a multitalented man."

He looked up, a pleased light in his eye. "Well, at least my choice of career had *some* side benefits, survival training among them."

She stepped behind him and rubbed his neck and shoulders with both hands as he finished stoking the fire. "I don't know. Surely some of those agents can't do what you've done for the past few days. You must be pretty special." Flirting with him was so much fun now that they were married.

He chuckled. "Hmmm. You could be right about that."

"Ugh. My hands feel gritty. I think I'll go in for a dip in the water." She danced a few steps away. "Coming?"

He winked saucily. "You betcha." One last glance at the fire had him frowning as he noticed it dying down, perhaps a bit too much. "I'll be right there, let me just make sure this is all set."

"Okay." She skipped down to the shoreline and dived in, relishing the coolness of the crystalline water and the feeling of the bubbles against her face. Even if she paid for it later with salt crusted on her skin, it was worth it.

She lingered underwater, eyes closed, pretending she was a mermaid waiting for her handsome prince. A distant, echoey shout reverberated to her ears and she surfaced...

...Only to find the ugly toothed snout of an immense saltwater crocodile pointed straight at her nose. A split-second realization that she was about to die a horrible death choked her deep in the throat as the beast opened its jaws for a bite. Or maybe it was the salt water in her lungs.

Her scrabbling feet found the bottom and she pushed for the shore, but the sharp teeth tore against her hip and she floundered. A steady stream of shouts grew closer and more discernible as suddenly Bryce was there next to her in the water.

"CARA!! MOVE!!" Metal flashed in the sun and then blood. Blood everywhere. Bryce had slashed at the soft pale underbelly of the croc with one of the knives they recovered from the booby trap. With his striking blow, he narrowly avoided the crushing jaws and slashing claws of the attacking predator.

She obeyed his command and moved, struggling out of the water and onto the hot sand. A warm crimson stream trickled down her leg and pain burst through her hip. She looked back, horror-stricken, unable to tear her gaze from the fight.

Bryce seemed enraged but calculating as he jabbed at the enormous reptile in what seemed to be strategic points, where it was most vulnerable. The water frothed around them.

Then the crocodile lay limp, Bryce emerging without a wound save for the scratch on his thigh from the animal's thrashing muscled tail. He sloshed onto the beach and collapsed next to her on the sand, cradling her in an embrace.

"Oh my God." He changed it to a prayer. "Oh God. Thank you for sparing her." Bryce cupped her cheek in his hand. "I thought I was losing you."

"I'm okay." She gasped out.

He didn't take her at her word, but swept her whole body with his gaze. He didn't miss the scratch on her hip, and quickly pressed one of his hands over the wound to stop the bleeding. "You-" He broke off, and she realized his whole body was trembling. "You are *not* okay – but you are *very* brave." He covered her mouth with his in a comforting kiss, warm but gentle.

At last they parted, needing air. She rested her head in the curve of his neck and shoulder, taking deep, slow breaths and trying to rid her lungs of the clogged, salty feeling.

"Where did it come from?" She asked, wondering how one moment she could be surrounded by nothing but pristinely clear water in the blue lagoon, the next face-to-face with Croczilla.

"It was up on the bank, among those logs." He pointed to one side of the circular lagoon. "When it heard you splash into the water, it slid down to check you out and decided you'd be dinner."

"And I would have been, if not for you and your blade." She sighed, a smile creasing her face for the first time since the attack. "My knight in shining armor."

"Sans the armor." He pulled himself upright and shook some of the water from his light-brown hair. "All right. Here's what we're gonna do. You keep your hand here-" He replaced his hand on her hip with hers. "I'm gonna go get you a bandage and make sure the fire hasn't died. And once I come back, we're gonna figure out how to roast that fellow for a crocodile-steak supper." He eyed the dragon he'd slain for her so gallantly, then gazed into her eyes again.

"Sounds fine. I'll be right here." She tried to reassure him with a purposefully calm expression and even tone.

He stood, then kneeled to kiss her once more, on the forehead this time. "Okay. I'll just be thirty seconds." Then he sprinted up the beach.

While he was gone, her gaze flitted to the reptile reposing half-in, half out of the water. The movement of the gentle tide made its tail curl back and forth for a second, sending a shiver down her arms.

The knife lay in the sand where Bryce had dropped it, now streaked with the crocodile's blood. When her husband came bounding back, he scooped it up and washed it, sheathing it in a belt tied around his waist. "From now on, I'm carrying this on my person at all times!"

After rinsing her blood away with stinging salt water, Bryce tenderly bandaged her leg with a piece of fabric torn from the hem of his t-shirt. It left him with a "crop-top", which he stored in the hut, probably never to wear again, deigning it too silly-looking.

"Now, honey, you rest while I go filet some steaks from yonder croc. We're both gonna need that red meat for sustenance."

The thought of consuming something that had wanted to eat *her* struck Cara as oddly ironic, but she nodded. While Bryce worked, she kept an eye on the fire and fed it a few pieces of wood.

A short while later, Bryce came back with several slabs of meat and they rigged a platform of hard stakes to lay it on, over the coals. Cara felt her revulsion fade as the meat slowly browned on the edges and began to smell savory and drip juice. She even cracked open a coconut to go with it using another of the knives. While they waited for it to cook, Bryce hung several pieces of meat, the flanks and sirloin, in the rafters of the hut to cure for later.

Bryce prayed over the meal when it was ready, thanking God for his mercy in protecting both of them and providing them with the nourishment in heartfelt words. When she opened her eyes, she noticed tears glistening in his own. He clasped one of her hands with his. "I love you." He said.

"Love you too, darling. Let's eat."

The sentiment fled from his face and he grinned. "Aye, and hearty too, for that thar meat will not be a-lastin' long." He donned a piratical accent and sank his teeth into his meat.

Cara did likewise and they ate their fill of the choice cuts of the crocodile, grilling several batches of meat, until they were both absolutely stuffed and couldn't eat another bite.

"Ugh. It's not bad, but eating that much meat at once is almost enough to make me to turn vegetarian." She wiped her fingers on a leaf 'napkin' and took one last swig of coconut water.

"Nuh-uh. You're never gonna get me to forsake bacon and beef in favor of tofu." Bryce laughed. "Just so you know that up front."

"Ha-ha. No worries, I'd never force such restrictions on you, dear husband." She looked up at the clouds, which for the past few hours had been stirring uneasily. "Do you think it might rain?"

He stood and scanned the darkening sky. "Hmm. That's not just nightfall. I think a storm is rolling in." His eyes danced. "But you know what that means..."

Hmm... She looked at her hubby's strong, muscular chest. "Being cooped up in the hut together?" She batted her eyelashes.

He guffawed. "That, and *fresh water!* Falling from the sky! You sit tight while I rig some rain containers." He squinted at the horizon. "With any luck, it'll provide us with drinking water, but *not* knock over our less-than-perfect hut."

"Yes, let's hope not."

Penny ran a hand through her tangled red ringlets. Hopeless. Until she could coax her hair back into submission with hot water, a wide-tooth comb, and conditioner, it reigned supreme in a wild mess. Aside from the wrinkles of stress on his forehead, Blake wasn't looking too bad after their long day of travel. *Not bad at all...* Penny jerked her brain back from admiring the pleasing symmetry of Blake's face and tried to focus on the action.

At the moment, they had a front-row seat to watch the agency taskforce scrambling to set up a search grid. They'd found satellite images of the boat that had drawn into shore near the time Bryce and Cara were abducted and tracked it out to a luxury cruiser – which had then led them a merry chase trying to track it through a myriad of tiny islands peppering the ocean. Then they lost it amid a bank of clouds from the rapidly forming tropical storm that threatened to put a damper on the search.

Two agents were charting a radius now of where the boat could have ended its dastardly voyage, while others coordinated the helicopters and coordinated with the coast guard. Agent Pearlwind kept a close eye on the weather and gave them updates every fifteen minutes. A continuous stream of backup kept arriving and being sent out in a full-out manhunt for, it seemed, everyone's favorite agent... Bryce Reynolds.

Her mind swimming from the buzz of activity in the room, Penny leaned back against what she thought was the wall and jumped when she realized Blake stood behind her. He caught her arm and drew her back next to him, bent low to whisper in her ear. "It's like an anthill in here."

"Yeah... it's crazy. But encouraging! I mean, with all this effort, surely we're going to find them, right?" She searched his expression for some reassurance.

He frowned and his mouth pulled slightly to the side. "I sure hope so, but nothing's for certain. At least they know what boat took them. Agent Spartan is checking all the slips in the harbors for a match in case the smaller boat got dumped anywhere nearby."

"What can we do? I feel so helpless." *And weak. And tired. And in need of a nice cup of tea. Yeah – that'd be good.*

He lifted his muscular shoulder in a shrug, and his eyes flashed uncertainty. "Don't know. I'm concerned about the storm – if it gets any stronger it'll achieve hurricane status."

Penny gulped down a cry of fear. *Cara, abducted, who knows where, in the middle of a hurricane?! She's supposed to be on her honeymoon!*

Blake looked at her and then put his arm around her shoulders. "It's gonna be ok." He whispered.

Angelwing turned from barking another order and her gaze caught on the two of them. She marched over and leaned close. "Look, guys. I don't know how much good you're going to be for the next few hours. Go get some sleep and report back in the morning."

Blake sighed, as if he didn't want to agree with what Angel was saying, but did. "All right." He looked at Penny. "I'll walk you back to your room."

She agreed, more than willing to have an escort-slash-bodyguard in a hotel where someone had been abducted just a few days before. Plus, she had a few bags of her favorite vanilla-mint tea in her suitcase and knew how to rig the hotel coffeepot to brew it.

At the door of her room, Blake stopped, looking as if he wanted to say something.

She tilted her head. "What is it?"

He leaned against the wall with one shoulder, turned towards her. "I just wanted to thank you for coming along. I still don't have any clue what I'm doing... but you make it better."

The happy-go-lucky personality she'd seen when she first met Blake had dropped, to reveal a more serious, caring side of him. It made her want to know more about this man who cared so deeply about his brother.

She could feel herself smile softly. "Well, I don't know what I'm doing either... so what are we doing here, Blake?"

132

He shook his head slowly. "I don't know."

"I'll tell you what we're doing…" She stepped closer and reached for his hands. "…Faking it." She tugged him into a waltz in the middle of the hallway, to a silent tune only they could hear. And they danced, just like they had at Cara and Bryce's wedding reception.

 He grinned, and she could feel him relax. Her worries melted like ice cream left out in the sun.

The sight of other guests approaching along the hallway made them stop, laughing quietly at how silly they must look.

Blake squeezed her hand before he let go. "Thanks, Penny."

"You're welcome." She looked down to hide her blushing smile, and unlocked her hotel door with the plastic key card. She looked over her shoulder. "I hope you get some great rest."

"You too." He waited until she'd successfully opened the door, then slipped his hands in his pockets and walked away. "Goodnight."

"Goodnight." She leaned against the solid door once it closed, feeling like it was a thick barrier between them. She slid the deadbolt closed, then stared at it.

What did I just do…? Logically, in her head, she knew Mason wasn't here anymore, he was in heaven. But her heart still ached from his absence. She felt almost traitorous.

A sigh drifted from her lips. Maybe this was one ailment a cup of tea *couldn't* cure... but she'd try it just the same.

After coaxing the coffeepot to perform a minor miracle and make some hot vanilla-mint tea, Penny wandered onto the balcony jutting out from her hotel room into the warm Hawaiian air. She wished she had her paints, so she could capture the view of the Oahu skyline and the ocean at night. The breeze felt like a whisper of Aloha – a word that could mean hello, I love you, or goodbye.

How poignant that is. Penny mused, cupping her tea with both hands and breathing in the fragrant steam. *You'd have to listen to the heart behind the word to understand its meaning.*

She looked up at the stars, looking like diamonds in a velvety sky. The glow from the pool lights down on the ground level couldn't obscure the brightest twinklers. She let out a long, long sigh.

"Lord, I know you're there. We haven't been on the best of terms lately... since Mason's death... and I'm sorry. But right now, two of your children that you love dearly – Cara and her husband, Bryce – are in need of your help." She closed her eyes. "Please, God. Please guide the searchers to them and let their location be made known. Keep them safe and let them be *found.*"

The words trailed away on the wind.

Midnight, and he was driving hours away from the station to a desolate location along the oceanfront. The only slight consolation was the happy Australian sheepdog next to him in the passenger seat of the truck, tongue lolling, sticking his head out the window so the breeze could ruffle his handsome mottled coat.

At least someone is enjoying this. Greg pushed the accelerator harder, all the while imagining what would happen if someone noticed his unexplained absence back at the ranch house. If challenged when he returned, he'd say the dog had been sick and he'd taken it to the vet. But after his close escape from being seen on the hidden submarine, his luck was stretched pretty thin.

There'd been a time when he hadn't believed in luck, but rather favor from the hand of the creator. But it had been a long time he'd been running on his own, and he wasn't sure what to do to get out of the rut.

One step at a time. Finish this, and then maybe he could go rebuild some of the bridges he'd burned.

Finally, he made it to the spot, double-checking it on his GPS device. Slammed the door of the truck and let the dog nose around in the bushes.

The whirring of approaching helicopter blades told him he was right on time. In a flat open space along the cliff, the driver parked the copter with pinpoint precision and a cloaked figure got out and paced towards him.

135

The familiar coffee-colored face was barely discernible in the darkness, but still had a calming effect on his tension. They shook hands, and he noticed that his old friend's grip had gotten… puffier.

"Eating too many doughnuts lately, Montrose?"

Monty's brown eyes twinkled above his bristly mustache. "I don't get the same amount of fresh air and exercise as you." He scratched the head of the sheepdog, which sniffed him in greeting, then wandered away, satisfied.

"I owe my physique to unruly steers and long hours in the saddle." He chuckled. "It's not the easiest way to keep in shape."

"Yes. Well, it was a huge concession to fly out here, Greg – if you only knew how many things I've got on my plate right now, you'd realize I have very little time for small talk."

It was so like Benjamin Montrose to cut straight to the heart of the matter. Greg clapped his hands together. "Right." Hesitated.

Monty frowned. "What did you do?"

"Uhh, well-"

"Greg! Out with it, man!"

"Okay, okay." He opened his mouth and it all came out. "Cooper has a submarine with the capability to launch the Tomahawk missile he got from a Serbian terrorist, and I think he's planning on sending it to America – but don't worry, I sabotaged the sub."

Montrose rolled his eyes. Blinked. "You did *what?!*" He threw his hands in the air and began pacing. "*This* is your problem! You are a loose cannon – you've been out here on your own too long." His voice rang with indignation. "I don't know how I'm ever going to bring you back in-"

He interrupted with a hand on Monty's arm. "Just hold on a minute, will ya? I bought us some time. I infected the submarine's computers with a virus that makes the launch impossible."

Monty grilled him with a stare that went straight to the back of his skull. "Are you telling me that Cooper will have to get a whole new computer system and install it in the sub? Or can he fix it?"

"That's the beauty of it. It looks fixable, so they'll waste hours – maybe even days – trying to repair it, but eventually they're going to have to install some new drives."

"Are you *sure?*"

"...99% sure."

"Not good enough." Monty groaned. "I do not need this right now..." He rubbed his face. "There are some situations, one in particular, that have me running on fumes right now." He looked at him, and something strange flashed through his eyes. Almost as if he was holding something pertinent back.

"Well... " Greg scuffed the toe of his boot in the dirt. "Wish that was all the news I had for you, but I've got one more thing, and it ain't good."

Montrose spread his hands in a motion of acceptance. "At this point, the day cannot get worse, so fire away."

"There are two people right now stranded on a deserted island that Cooper owns. It's some kind of revenge thing."

Monty's eyes widened to the size of golf balls, with dark-brown pupils in the center, and went completely still. "Who are they?"

"I don't know all the details, just picked up some chatter from the hired goons, but it seems it's a husband and wife that Cooper has a grudge against." He wondered why this tidbit of info had captured Montrose's attention so strongly. *I mean, sure, the man is compassionate, but... who are they?*

He stepped closer and poked a finger into Greg's plaid shirt. "Listen closely. I want every bit of intel you can gather on those people, you got that? Everything. I don't care what kind of risk you have to take to get it."

"Yes sir." When the man spoke like that, no one crossed him.

"Fine." His expression smoothed. "But please, be careful. We don't need any more unsanctioned moves like you took with the sub. I'd like to see you in one piece at the end of all this."

"Me too, Monty." *I have some redeeming to do... and hopefully, a family waiting for me.* He couldn't bring himself to ask how

Dawn and little Bethy and the boys were doing. The pain was too sharp. Like shards of broken glass.

"Here, take this." Monty drew a satellite phone from inside his jacket and handed it to him. "No more driving off to the pub, just find somewhere on the ranch where you won't be overheard."

Greg nodded. That would make things simpler. "'Bout time I had some fresh tech. Thanks."

Montrose's own phone buzzed. One glance at the screen and he had done an about-face, headed back to the helicopter. "No more time! Stay smart, keep me informed! I'm out of here!" He had to shout over the rotors for Greg to hear him.

"I'll be careful!" *They won't catch me. I'm the gingerbread man.*

Markdown felt relieved when the gruff African-flavored voice of his boss came through the phone at last. "Montrose here!"

"Monty – good grief, are you on a helicopter?" His boss had to shout over the whirring noise in the background.

"YES!"

"...Oh. Right. Anyway – we had to let you know there's been a setback – a tropical storm is forming over the search grid and we're having difficulty with the S&R."

"A hurricane! Just what the doctor ordered!" Monty used a few words he only let slip at the end of a very bad day. "Listen. I need you to split off some of your men and send them to the coordinates I'm sending you. I've just been investigating Mr. Cooper Farnsworth and it seems he has gotten ahold of a Tomahawk missile – and you're closer to the location right now than anyone back at HQ."

"He has a nuke? Oh, *Great*."

"My sentiments exactly. I've just talked to the Gingerbread Man and he's told me Cooper is holding a man and a woman on his private deserted island. Get the location of that, ASAP. It may be owned under a subsidiary company of his, not his name directly."

Wonder, hope, dread all churned together inside of Markdown at these words. He hardly knew what to respond to first, the fact that they might have a location on Bryce and Cara, or the fact that Monty had been talking to the Gingerbread Man... more myth and legend than reality, an operative that had gone dark more than a decade ago after doing some of the most successful espionage the Agency had ever seen. *Or* the fact that his best friend might be fighting for his life on a deserted island.

He chose one. "Do you think it's them?"

"Maybe. It's our best lead at the moment, so we're gonna chase it." The whirring background noise hadn't diminished. "In the meantime, keep an eye on Cooper's ranch via satellite!"

"Yes sir!" The line went dead, but he had never felt more alive.

CHAPTER EIGHT

Discoveries and Disclosures

Dawn on the Australian outback never ceased to invigorate Cooper. Standing on the veranda, swigging a cup of black coffee and breathing in the fresh, raw morning air, things couldn't be more perfect.

First things first. Breakfast, then a meeting with the men, and then a nice little present sent over to knock the cursed state of California right into the ocean. He grinned. *Sounds like a full day.*

The sheepdog lay curled up on the steps, asleep. It'd probably had a late night out chasing nocturnal critters. The rest of the ranch house also lay silent, not yet awake to face the day.

Suddenly he had a fancy to see his most prized treasure – the Black Swan. Did she still repose silently in her chamber? He set off with the almost bowlegged stride of somebody used to riding horseback – for in his youth, he'd done a fair bit of cattle mustering.

Being so many years older than Jack, fifteen to be exact, he'd been more like a second father than a brother to him, especially since theirs was a lazy drunkard. On his mother's deathbed, Cooper had promised to watch out for the little boy with the gap-toothed grin and mop of curly hair. That little boy had grown into a spoiled young man, who started running with the wrong crowd of jackaroos.

Nothing he could say would convince Jack to stop and change his behavior, until one day he'd received one of those unemotional, chilling notices – "We regret to inform you…"

His good mood soured, Cooper snarled to himself, kicking aside a clod of dirt as he stomped onwards to the garage to get his truck. Too far to walk to the grotto.

Poor Jack. His life cut short by some dunderheaded special agent with a point to make. He would never forgive fate for dealing that blow.

He yanked open the truck door, thumped into the seat, revved the motor, and tore out of the open garage, caring not that he'd probably woken up all the hired men sleeping in the bunkhouse adjacent to it.

He stewed all the way out to the coast, but smiled to himself once he reached the grotto's entrance and parked. He got out and gently thumped the truck door closed. Walked with soft steps towards his treasure, like a parent approaching a cradle.

The men guarding the submarine nodded respectfully as he stepped aboard. He wandered the narrow hall, admiring the cold steel. She was ready to inflict some reckoning.

Cooper entered the control room, pleased at the sight of all the computers and dials. He was unfamiliar with this kind of technology – had only recently switched to using a smartphone, in fact – so he called one of the men over. "Is everything in ordah for the launch, mate?"

"Yes sir." The man saluted. What did he think he was, a general?

"Don't salute me, and double-check it. Royt now."

"Yes, sir. One moment." The man's fingers flew over the touch-screen keyboard, then he froze. Tapped a few more keys. He turned his head towards Cooper. His expression reminded him of a wallaby he'd once trapped in the outback, who would rather be anywhere but there.

Dread coursed through him, stronger than his morning coffee had been. *"WHAT IS IT?!"* He gripped the man by his collar and jerked his face inches from his own.

"Ah-ah-I'm afraid there's something wrong-"

"WHAT'S WRONG?!"

The seaman gulped, clutching at Cooper's hands at his throat. "It's the launch software – it seems to be corrupted-"

"WHY?!" He was roaring like a wildfire and couldn't seem to stop. "How could this *possibly* have happened?!" His aussie accent got even twangier when he was angry.

Another uniformed seaman stepped a bit closer and spoke up. "If you'll put him down, sir, he'll try to figure it out for you."

"Do *NOT* tell me what to do!" Cooper ordered, but he released the man, leaving sharp wrinkles in his shirt.

The man gulped, still shaking, and turned his gaze to the computer. "It's been infected somehow, with a virus, looks like. Otherwise the processing codes-"

"*How*?! How did that happen?" He spouted off a blue streak of cursing before the seaman could answer.

When he stopped for breath, the man hurriedly gasped out "I'll have to run diagnostics on it-"

Cooper's rage had cooled and hardened now, like a lava flow. "You do that, mate, and you had better fix it, because if you don't..." He stared straight into the pupils of the man's eyes... "I'll kill you."

Apparently, the man believed this sincere threat, because he went white as a ghost. He whirled to face the computer and set to work at lightning speed. This calmed some of Cooper's fury.

"I'll leave you blokes to it." He stalked out of the room.

Nobody dared to speak to him on his way back to the truck, so the look on his face must have been foreboding indeed. *I'll kill them. When I find out who is responsible for this, they. will. suffer.*

Torture. That's what it had been having to walk away and leave Penny last night after their impromptu dance in the hallway. *She is so...* Blake ran his hand through his hair, sweeping it away from his face. He couldn't put into words how Penny made him feel, but he did know that he'd wanted to stay with her and never leave.

The resort's breakfast buffet could not have been more splendid, but his appetite was next to nothing. Blake stared at his plate. The steaming scrambled eggs, glistening strips of bacon, fresh, juicy pineapple – all of it wasted on him. Besides his newfound feelings for Penny, he couldn't stop thinking about Bryce and Cara. How were they living right now? Maybe tied up somewhere? Beaten? Starving? He nudged the plate away and leaned his chin on his fist.

A soft hand dropped on his shoulder. "Hey, why is a big hunk of a guy like you ignoring a plate of food looking like *that*?" It was a woman's voice – low and mellow.

He turned to see Agent Angelwing looking down at him, compassion in her maple-brown eyes.

"Uh, guess I'm just worried." He shrugged.

She shook her head like she could see right through him. Probably could, after working with Bryce. "You are so much like your brother." She bit her lip, studying his face. "A little taller, hair a little darker, but you two are more alike than some twins I've met."

It felt good to hear it again. People had said as much his entire life. "Well, he'd likely disagree... Bryce would say he's the 'older and wiser' one, while I'm the little kid who never took anything seriously."

Angel frowned. "I know Bryce is the type to take on responsibility and watch out for others, but all he's ever told us about you is that you're the handsome one in the family." She laughed.

Relief settled on him like a warm blanket. *Bryce never complained about his goofy kid brother? Even after all the times I caused him grief with my easygoing – okay – sometimes-lazy, habits?* He blinked, hard, willing the tears to go back from whence they came. "I know he thought I didn't care about things as much as he did. But that's not true. I just didn't know how to deal with stuff, so I shrug it off."

Angel gripped the back of the chair next to him and leaned forward slightly. "Time to deal, Blake. Bryce isn't here. You're gonna have to step up and be the man." She looked back towards the door to the dining room behind him. "There are people counting on you… one pretty girl in particular." She pointed to his plate. "So eat your food and get a grip." She winked. "Gotta scoot. See ya later."

As she walked away, he swiveled to see Penny approaching, a little bounce in her step. She wore shorts and a bright yellow tunic with white embroidery, and someone had bestowed a lei crafted from purple orchids around her neck. A grin found its way to his face and he stood to welcome her. "Good morning."

She opened her arms for a quick hug, which both shocked and thrilled him. "Good morning!" She plopped down at the table, a bit breathless. "I must have overslept. What are we going to do today?"

He sat, but glanced at the open space on the table in front of her. "Well, you might want to eat something first."

She looked down. "Oops! Gosh yeah, I'm starving – hang on a sec!" She popped back up and skipped to the buffet line.

He couldn't hide his grin as he watched her. Penny was such a ray of sunshine – despite her sad story of the fiancé she'd lost. What a girl. Nothing like the ones always chasing him.

Boy, it had been a while since he thought about Chelsea – a pouty blonde in the youth class at church. The first girl he'd 'liked', and told, had gone and bragged about it to her whole gaggle of girlfriends, and he'd overheard. And promptly told her off. She'd only wanted his attention for the popularity it would bring, not because she returned his feelings. Ever since, he'd held himself aloof from all female kind besides his mom and sister.

Until now.

Penny bounced back to the table with a plate heaped with goodies. "Oh wow, I didn't realize how much I took – trust me, I have a super high metabolism, or I would look like a whale." She apologized with an abashed expression on her freckled face.

"Hey, go for it. When the food is this awesome, that's the time to enjoy it." *Actually, it's refreshing to see a girl who doesn't stress over calories.* He pulled his plate closer again and picked up his fork.

She noticed. "You didn't have to wait for me! Goodness! Did it get cold?"

"Due to the pre-warmed plate, nope... and I wasn't waiting. I just couldn't eat until I got a talking-to from Angel – and now the sight of you." He winked. "Suddenly I have an appetite."

Her cheeks pinked, and she focused on unfolding her napkin. "Should we pray for our meal?"

"Sure." He reached for her hand, and this time she placed it in his without hesitation. He gave thanks for the five-star food and prayed for protection for Bryce and Cara.

"Amen" she echoed after him, and then tasted a bite of the coconut cream puffs. "These are delicious!"

He was glad to see her in such good spirits – it was rubbing off on him. "Did you sleep well last night?"

She nodded, mouth full, then swallowed and patted her lips with the linen napkin. "Surprisingly, I did. I prayed about it... for the first time in a while, actually... and felt so much better afterwards. It doesn't make sense, but – yeah."

"Good." He smiled, then tried the bacon. Perfectly crisp and full of flavor. *Wait... the first time in a while?* "So... how often would you say you pray?"

She looked taken aback, then poked at her papaya chunks with her fork. "Well... it's funny you should ask. A few months ago, I would have said every day. Without fail. But then..." Her gaze shifted away and she stared into the distance.

But then the guy she loved was torn away from her.

"Ah." The word was spoken low, with feeling. He sympathized with this brave, colorful, spunky girl who kept her hurt locked inside where no one could see it.

He pulled out his phone. "I need to share something with you."

Now she looked downright confused, but spooned her yogurt in silence while he found what he was looking for. He plugged in his earbuds and held one out to her. The other he popped into his ear. "It's a song."

She slipped it into one of her own dainty ears and listened. Danny Gokey sang along with a tinkling piano backdrop.

"Shattered – like you've never been before. The life you knew... in a thousand pieces on the floor..."

Her eyes widened and she nodded, as if she could relate.

He prayed inwardly, hoping this was from God and not just an exceedingly stupid idea.

The chorus began and the music swelled hopefully.

Tell your heart to beat again

Close your eyes and breathe it in

Let the shadows fall away

Step into the light of Grace

Yesterday's a closing door

You don't live there anymore

Say goodbye to where you've been

And tell your heart to beat again

Her eyes filled with tears and she pressed her lips together, but when he began to speak she held up a hand and looked away, listening to the whole song until it was finished. One single tear made its way down her cheek at the end, but then she took a deep breath.

"Thank you." The look on her face – he knew healing had begun.

He wrapped up his earbuds and put the phone away. "He lost his wife to cancer."

"Wow." Penny wiped at her eyes and ate a whole cream puff in one bite. When she'd swallowed, she said "I can't imagine the heartbreak of slowly losing someone like that. And then to be able to write a song saying it's time to begin again?" She looked as if she was holding back a sob.

"Yeah." He held her hand in his. "Your heart will heal, Penny-girl."

Her face squeezed up and she closed her eyes, as if the kindness was too much. "Thanks, Blake." She opened her eyes and smiled bravely. "You are so sweet."

"Hey, what can I say? I try." He winked saucily at her in an effort to cheer her up.

She laughed, so he guessed it worked.

And then his phone jingled, signaling a text. It was from Agent Markdown.

[Mark Benson]: BIG DEVELOPMENT. MEET US IN THE SEARCH HQ ROOM. HURRY.

Cara awoke again, this time to an extremely loud crash of thunder booming overhead. After their huge meal of roast croc, they'd slept a long time, waking late in the morning. The storm had moved in with raging fury and Bryce had dashed out to collect the rainwater from the containers he had rigged. The water streamed off the roof of their thatched hut in sheets, and Cara had used it as an outdoor shower – finally able to wash some of the sandy, salty stiffness from her super-long hair. Then she'd braided it into a rope and tied itself in a knot at the end to keep it out of the way. But the ferocity of the storm had driven them inside, to fall asleep again in a wet heap.

She picked up her head and looked out of the hole they used for a door. The sky was an ashen white, grey banks of clouds blackening it in speeding swirls. She was glad to have an abundance of fresh water for the first time in days, but she was so frightened by the sheer force of the storm. The foliage thrashed about, wind-torn, water pouring from the leaves. The roar of crashing raindrops and gale-force winds drowned out any other noise.

Her husband sensed her movement and opened his eyes. Like her, the first thing he did was sit up and look outside. "Man!" He shouted to be heard. "I think we have a hurricane on our hands!"

"That's bad, right?!" She shouted nearly in his ear so he could understand.

He grimaced. "Well – it's not good!"

Great. I hope we don't get killed by this storm after surviving everything else!

The hut creaked in protest as the wind tugged at it roughly.

Bryce frowned and his eyes darted from the view of the outdoors to the walls, to the crocodile meat hanging from the rafters, to their meager supplies stacked along the driest side. He pushed to his feet. "I think we'd better-" the last words were lost in the noise. It sounded like "Ketchup".

"WHAT?" she shrieked over the keening wind.

He turned and looked straight at her. "PACK UP." He shouted, but she could hardly hear him even though a tendon jerked in his neck from the effort. If not for half-reading his lips, she would have missed it.

"OK!" She helped as they wrapped up all their things in green packages made from wide banana palm leaves. The meat, the tools, extra fabric from ripped t-shirts, anything that could potentially help them in their struggle for survival was carefully collected.

Once the supplies were stacked in a pile, ready for anything, Bryce looked at her and made a "come-here" gesture with his hand, then spread his arms wide.

Warmth flooding through her, she lunged towards him and nestled in his embrace. He stroked her wet hair and put his lips close to her ear. "We're gonna be ok. But I don't think our hut will hold much longer. We'll move to a cave in the side of the mountain – there's gotta be a safer place to ride out this storm." He didn't have to shout so loudly in this position, which allowed a soothing note in his voice.

She hugged him tighter, trying not to freak at the thought of leaving their little makeshift shelter, unstable as it was. But she would follow him to the ends of the earth, so she nodded against his chest.

"Good." He kissed her warmly then grinned, a proud light in his eye. "That's my girl!"

She smiled into his face, hoping she looked as brave as he thought her to be. *What would I do without him? He's saved our lives every moment, this whole time.*

Bryce made her carry the lightest of the bundles while he grasped the other two in one arm. Hands tightly clutching each other, they made a break for it.

Water doused them like someone was deliberately pouring buckets over their heads, and the uneven jungle terrain slashed at their shoeless feet and bare calves. Without Bryce's steadying hand, she would have fallen many times over.

They fought their way through the blinding rain towards the mountain. Progress was slower than their day of exploration, but eventually they forged through the jungle and made it to the base of the mount. Rocks now studded the ground and sides of the hill.

Then Bryce shook her hand and pointed with his chin. There, a darker spot amongst the wind-whipped brush. A gaping hole in the side of the hill.

They reached it and he was the first to get inside, checking it out as best as he could with no light. He nodded and pulled her inside with him. She had to stoop to enter, but not far. Good thing neither of them had claustrophobia, though.

The smell of damp earth greeted them as they dropped the bundles and collapsed to their knees, panting from the exertion.

"Mmmmhhhrrrrr. Mmmhhhrr." The deep, grumbling roar echoed from deep inside the cave.

NO. Oh God, no.

Bryce ripped open a palm-leaf package and had a blade gripped in his hand even before he was cognizant of what he was actually doing. *Thank God for reflexes.*

He crouched protectively in front of his wife, who was still gasping in shock. Everything seemed to move a little slower in crisis mode when his brain was processing at lightning speeds.

154

Could there possibly be a lion inside this cave with them? Lurking deep in the blackness at the end?

He replayed the roar again in his head, studying, analyzing. The noise had been slightly tinny. And why would a lion be roaring in a cave in the middle of a storm? That roar sounded like it was meant to be a long-distance call, marking territory, perhaps. If a lion was truly trapped between them and daylight, wouldn't it growl instead?

This is just plain weird. "I'm gonna check this out." He found Cara's arm with his other hand and squeezed it comfortingly. "Stay here. And grab a knife."

"No! Bryce, don't!" Her voice trembled and her soft, slim hands clasped around his bicep, tugging him back to her.

"Trust me. I have a hunch." He kept his gaze focused in the direction of the lion sounds, but side-hugged her with one arm and kissed the top of her head. "I'll be right back."

She exhaled, still sounding scared, but she let go and he could hear her rummaging around for another weapon.

What a woman I've married. His heart thrummed with joy for a moment. A brief one.

"Mmmmhhhrrrrr. Mmmhhhrr."

This time he got an even better fix on where the sound was coming from and crept forward in the wet, mushy dirt on the floor of the cavern. It grew drier as he made it farther in, but the light dimmed. He stopped for a few seconds to let his eyes adjust.

No eye-shine from feline eyeballs could be seen. If there was a big cat, it was either closing its eyes or turned away from him.

He followed the cave until he could stand upright. A larger room at the back opened up. No tunnels branching off from it. There was, however, a crack somewhere up above that was letting a trickle of water and a thin beam of light in.

Bryce carefully looked around. No sign – or smell – of lions anywhere. But there was a strange box at the back of the cave – too small to contain even a baby lion cub. He walked up to it and realized there were holes spread along the side – it was a speaker.

He touched the black cube and turned it around. The back had a panel that popped open to reveal computerized controls. He laughed out loud. *Cooper was trying to scare us with animal sounds? The man is ridiculous!*

Just then, the roars started up again, making his eardrums crackle with the proximity of the loud noise. He hastily punched a few buttons and shut it off.

"Darling, I found the source of our scare." He called back through the cave. "Come here."

Her pattering footsteps were heard before he could make out the gleam of her blond head, darker and wetter than usual.

Then her creamy oval face with the high cheekbones and sparkling gray eyes.

"What was it?" She looked around at the floor and sides of the cave, incredulous.

"This." He hefted the box in his hands. "It's similar to a device we use sometimes in the Agency. It can be programmed to emit any number of noises or background sounds – but we generally use them for signaling messages."

"Oh, wow!" Cara's forehead wrinkled. "What's it doing here?"

"I think it's been deliberately stuck here to amplify out of this cave, across the whole island." He tapped the keypad. "Let's see if we can make it say something else."

"Like what? "Help Us", perhaps?" Cara bit her lip.

"I was thinking Morse Code, SOS. Three short blips, three long beeps, three short blips. We'll have to wait until the storm abates, though. Nobody's going to hear this over a hurricane."

They still had no guarantee that anyone was out there listening.

"Listen to this." Agent Markdown scrolled down his touchscreen and zoomed in on an image of a Serbian man entering a public restroom. "We just got a tip from Interpol that this known terrorist, Nebo Hadrabi, and Cooper Farnsworth were observed together by one of Interpol's operatives. They had a meeting three days ago."

Blake and Penny were in the search HQ room with the other agents, who all seemed positive as they gathered around the conference table over three boxes of ham-and-pineapple pizza. Blake took that as a good sign.

"He's definitely up to something." Angelwing nodded. "We're keeping an eye on his property on the Australian coastline. If he makes a move, we'll get him."

"Sorry – Cooper who? What does this have to do with Bryce and Cara?" Blake broke in, hoping for an explanation.

Angelwing frowned. "We believe he could be the one who ordered Bryce and Cara's abduction."

"Goodness, why?!" Penny gasped.

"It's a long story, but in short, Cooper blames Bryce for the death of his younger brother, Jack Farnsworth. But it wasn't Bryce's fault-" Markdown cut himself off and shook his head. "Anyway, what's relevant is that we have a suspect and a lead to chase."

Agent Spartan chuckled. "Yeah, thanks to the Gingerbread Man."

"The what now?" Penny turned towards the man, confusion stamped on her face.

"The man, the myth, the legend." Spartan smirked.

"Quiet, Sparty." Angelwing barked.

Spartan nodded and quietly went back to his work.

Angelwing and Markdown looked at each other, a silent conversation passing between their eyes. Mark nodded.

"He's a special agent for I.C.E. – that's us. The Inernational Counterintelligence & Espionage Agency." Angelwing shuffled the papers in her hands. "He was amazing, ten years ago. Then poof, he was gone without a trace, but last night our boss said he'd talked with him."

Penny looked interested. He was too. "Fascinating. So the Gingerbread guy gave you the intel on this Cooper fellow?"

"Apparently. But whatever the source, it's a step in the right direction." Markdown seemed done pursuing that line of discussion. "There's also some bad news to accompany the good."

Blake groaned. "What?"

"The tropical storm has reached hurricane status and been christened "Damaris" – and it's majorly hampering the efforts of the search crew. The helicopters are grounded and the coast guard all but immobilized."

"Darn." Penny crossed her arms, hiding behind them like a barbed-wire fence.

"Trust us. We're doing everything we can." Angelwing tried to reassure them.

159

I think it's time we left. Penny looked like she needed a distraction. "Well, thanks very much for keeping us in the loop." Blake reached for Penny's arm and moved towards the door. "We'll be around if you need us for anything."

Markdown nodded. "Sure thing."

As he and Penny walked out and through the ritzy lobby, Blake pondered those words. *Sure thing – is anything sure right now?*

They walked out the doors and past the scuba gear shack.

We don't even know if we're going to see Bryce and Cara alive again.

The thought struck through his soul like a dart from a speargun.

What a day. Cooper felt as if a tight cord inside him had been snipped, releasing the horrible tension. If it wasn't for his frighteningly smart personal assistant, Samir, they could have wasted days trying to repair those corrupted computer drives on the Black Swan.

Samir had briefly examined the malware that was installed and announced the whole thing had to go, start fresh. The new drives would arrive in approximately seven hours, and then had to be reinstalled. For now, he and Samir relaxed in the dining room with two crystal glasses and a bottle of deep, spicy red Syrah wine made from Australian grapes to accompany the wild game killed on the property. His wife had gone to her room with "a headache" – *more likely to read one of those cheap novels she enjoys.*

"Samir, good on ya for your work today." He tipped his glass to the man. "Well done."

Samir's eyes glittered with pride. "Thank you, Sah." His thick Egyptian accent coated his speech. Very different from Cooper's own Aussie twang. But complimentary. Like the wine and the meat.

"I haven't felt this pleased since we dropped off the newlyweds on the deserted island." He laughed, and sighed contently. "Wondah how they're doin' out there. More than likely, they're long dead, but if they've worked hahd at it, they could be hanging on by a thread."

Samir nodded. "My guess is they have died in each other's arms."

"Hmm, you could be right. I should have separated them, that sounds fah too cozy a death for the likes of Bryce and Cara Reynolds."

A chill penetrated straight down into his gut at the sound of his son's name from his boss's lips. Shock at the fact that his little boy had grown up and gotten married was drowned out by the realization that Bryce could have perished at the hand of this villain. Unless by some miracle, he and his new wife had survived.

Greg shifted closer to the dining room door, which was open just a crack and emitted a faint glow of light into the dim hallway of the ranch house. Soft carpet underfoot cushioned his step.

"You are right, Sah." Samir's harsh voice grated on his ears from the dining room. "But they may be having trouble with the hurricane over them right now."

Just then, a terrible scratchy wriggling sensation in his pants cuff made Greg jerk stiffly. Soundlessly, he kicked a lizard out of his pants leg, withholding even the slightest grunt of surprise or disgust, but the reptile landed with a skittering thud against the baseboard.

Silence stretched long in the dining room. Greg fled, soundlessly sprinting down the hall until he was in the kitchen. He heard someone coming down the hall after him and he didn't have time to make it out the back door. So he opened the fridge and stared inside as if searching for something to eat, and willed his racing heartbeat to slow down.

Mere seconds later, Samir eased his bulk through the doorway and glared down at him from eyes like black slits. "I know it was you."

He looked up and slammed the fridge closed. "What was me?"

Samir clenched his big fists and flexed his arms, and suddenly he looked about the same size as the fridge. "You were listening just now, outside the dining room. And I think you were the one who tampered with the sub."

"You're crazy, man." Greg smoothed his facial muscles into a blank canvas of innocence. Spread his hands wide. "I wasn't listening to anything but my grumbling stomach – I'm starved." He tilted his head to the side. "What sub? A sub sandwich?"

The henchman narrowed his already slitted eyes until Greg wondered how the man could still view him. "Don't try to fool me. I know more about you than you think."

Though a quiver of nervousness squirmed through him – afraid of what Samir might know – he rolled back his shoulders and joined the squint war, lowering his eyelids to half-mast. "I don't like your tone, my friend. And if it's integrity you want to compare, how about the little birdie who keeps dipping into Cooper's funds when he's not aware of it? Your already ample paycheck has gotten plumper the last few months and I didn't hear anything about you getting a raise."

Samir's bronzed face turned a pale yellow and he took a step back, then sneered. "There's no way you can prove this."

Greg opened the fridge again and rummaged around for the ingredients for a sub sandwich, which suddenly sounded delicious. "Ah, but numbers are such nice, solid things. So are paper trails and bank statements." He stood upright again, hands full of lunch meat, sliced cheese, and a jar of vegemite. "I wouldn't go whistle-blowing on me if your own nose isn't clean, Samir."

Greg calmly went about making his sandwich and ignored the glowering expression on Samir's face until the man stopped bluffing and left with a huff.

But he didn't breathe easy until Samir was gone, and with him, the threat of exposure.

I've gotta be more careful, or I'm bound to get caught. But is that even a possibility, with the safety of my country and my own son on the line?

He took the sandwich back to his room and ate half of it in about three ravenous bites. He needed the fuel for the work ahead of him. Clenching his jaw, the grief and horror rushed through him in waves. Pounding. Breaking.

Bryce is out there, somewhere. I know it. He can't be dead, he just can't – and his new wife, too. He wanted to meet her, to know the woman who had captured his son's heart. *He's a man now – and he made it to manhood without me.* The thought stung like a swarm of hornets.

And then a greater pain. *Montrose. He knew. He KNEW that Bryce and – what was her name, Cara? – were out on that island. And he didn't tell me. That's what he was holding back.*

He shoved the rest of the sandwich in the rubbish bin next to his desk, and pulled out his sat phone. Stood, paced to the door, locked it. Grabbed an old sweatshirt and wrapped it around his head and arms and slid underneath his bed for soundproofing.

Dialed Monty's number.

His ally and faithful contact picked up on the third ring. "Is that you, Ginger?"

He held his words to the pitch of a choked whisper. Being overheard could mean the end. "Why didn't you tell me?"

"Beg pardon?"

"Bryce."

"Oh. Because you would have flown off the handle as you are no doubt doing right now. We'll find him." A moment of silence. "How in blazes did you learn about Bryce?"

It was getting hot wrapped in his soundproofing sweatshirt. "Overheard Cooper and his right-hand thug. Monty, the missile launch software is back online. They replaced the drives sooner than I expected."

Monty swore and he heard sounds of panicked shuffling. "No! This can NOT be happening!"

"It is. I've gotta stop him-"

"You certainly will not. Get outta there, do you hear me? I am not losing the best agent I ever had *now* after hiding you for ten years. Head to Canberra and an extraction team will pull you out."

"Like that's happening." He pulled a 'Montrose' and hung up on his boss after his last sarcastic whisper. The phone almost immediately lit up with an incoming call from the I.C.E. Agency headquarters – Monty calling back – but he ripped the battery out of the phone and killed the power.

No. way. I'm not leaving this fight now.

CHAPTER NINE

Boats, Boys and Bombs

A hush fell over the Search HQ room as the dark menacing shadow of the submarine edged out of the cove and slipped into the sea. It had only been on their satellite imagery for the briefest moment in time before it submerged into the ocean depths, but that was enough to strike fear in the hearts of all ten agents crowded around the high-definition screen.

Angelwing recovered first. "All right! Now we know." her terse statement broke the silence, startling a few of the frozen agents. "There's an active threat moving towards us, people, and we need to alert the mainland and send a force to intercept that sub. Let's get moving!"

Her husband pulled her aside for a confab while the rest of the team went into action mode. "It looks like watching Cooper's station paid off."

Angel blew out a frustrated breath, releasing some of the tension. "Yeah, but we've gotta stop that sub or we're toast. There's no way to barricade off the entire pacific ocean between us and Australia."

"We'll find it. Even if they're out of sonar range and off-grid, we'll send everything we've got at it. I believe SEAL Team 9 is in the area." He touched her arm. "We can send them in below the water, and with the coast guard above –"

Angel shook her head. "It's still a lot of water. They could easily slip through our ranks. We are going to have to disable the missile remotely, from wherever Cooper Farnsworth is planning to hit the kill switch."

Markdown pressed his lips into a thin line. "You're right." He whirled away and grabbed a free laptop. "Let me finish tracking down the location of Cooper's island. That's what I was doing when we got the alert that the sub was moving."

"Good. Once we have that, we can actually move – and get out of this blasted hotel conference room."

Mark clicked, typed, clicked once more. "Got it. The coordinates are 13 degrees South, 163 degrees West."

She peered over his shoulder. "Wow, it's a little one, and about halfway between Hawaii and Australia."

"What's halfway between Hawaii and Australia?" Penny's voice broke in from behind them.

Markdown and Angelwing turned to see Penny and Blake standing in the doorway, looking like they'd just finished a swim in the hotel pool – Penny was still toweling off her hair.

"Bryce and Cara. On a deserted island." Mark answered, before Angel could stop him.

"Oh my gosh!" – "What?!" Penny and Blake simultaneously reacted to the bombshell he'd dropped on them and ran forward to look at the screen.

Angelwing sighed. "Guess you might as well know. Yes, we believe we've found it. Cooper Farnsworth owns this island and we have intel suggesting that he is holding Bryce and Cara there. But it doesn't guarantee anything."

"We've gotta go get them!" Blake's eyes blazed. "Even if I have to grab a boat and do it myself!"

"There's no need for that, we'll be joining you on that mission." Angel indicated herself and her husband.

"What about the storm?" Penny looked unsure. "Is it still gaining strength?"

"No, it's weakening — and that's the first piece of good news we've had in a long time." Markdown smiled tightly. "But it's still hovering right over these small islands, dumping rain and smashing winds. Getting in and out of there will mean taking our lives into our hands."

"Let's investigate." Angel grabbed her black jacket and zipped it up. "If you're coming with us, you'd better hurry. ETD is in ten minutes."

"We are." Blake and Penny answered as one, glanced at each other, and shared a quick smile before they darted out the door, probably to change out of their swimsuits.

"So are we leaving without them?" Markdown asked as soon as they were out of earshot.

Angel grinned. "Tempting. But I promised. So no, they're coming with us."

"Seriously?"

She pulled him close to her, face-to-face, and dropped her voice to a low murmur. "Put yourself in their place. If it was us, wanting to help Bryce and Cara, would you let anything stop you from going?"

He reluctantly nodded. "You're right." He took advantage of the close proximity and dropped a kiss on her mouth. "Love you."

"Love you too, hubs." She slipped out of his grasp before they could provide the other agents in the room with any more entertainment. "Let's go get 'em."

Greg raced down the dirt road heading to the grotto, throwing caution to the wind, though he kept nervously glancing in his rear-view mirror. If he could just make it there before it launched – it looked deserted. He slammed the brakes and swerved to a stop. Ejected himself from the car with the motor still running. Sprinted to the hole in the ground and ran down the tunnel.

Gone.

The submarine had vanished, leaving an empty grotto with light at the end reflecting on the water like a black mirror. Only two small craft remained in the entire cavern – a powerful speedboat and a pointy cigarette racing boat.

NO! Greg sank to his knees, and the gritty gravel ground against his jeans. *I'm too late.* There was no way to stop the missile launch now unless he could force Cooper to call it off –

"Well, if it isn't my trusty foreman." Cooper's sardonic twang echoed down the tunnel behind him. "But what could he be doin' down heah?"

Greg stood, but was halted by a command from his unworthy employer. "No sudden moves, mate. Slowly."

He pivoted at a snail's pace until he was staring at Cooper Farnsworth's lined face with the cruel mouth held in the perpetual twist. And behind him, Samir, with the smuggest of smirks, clutching a semi-automatic rifle to his chest, aimed directly at Greg.

Well. This doesn't look so great. I've got no good reason to be here besides sabotaging the sub again. None.

"He is the one responsible for the sabotage, Sah. I know it." Samir stared at him with eyes full of triumph, as if he knew he'd won. Then he delivered the final blow. "And I found a listening device that he planted in your hat. I discovered it when you asked me to repair the cracked band."

Woah. Been saving that piece of information, have you? Greg swallowed down a bubble of panic.

Cooper's face purpled and puffed, pure hatred popping out his eyes. He lunged at Samir and grabbed for the gun. "Gimme that! I'm gonna kill 'im! I'm gonna kill 'im, the little sabotaging sneak!"

Samir, taken aback, tangled with Cooper instead of cleanly handing the gun to him, and Greg took advantage of the three seconds of confusion. He dived into the black water and kicked off his shoes, striking out for the other side of the grotto where the boats were moored.

Underwater, bullets plunged on either side of him as he clawed his way through the wet darkness, sending thin trails of bubbles surfaceward. He made sure to close his fingers so his hands formed paddles, and swam with all his might in a straight line.

The gunfire stopped, and he waited four heartbeats before daring to come up for a breath. In a split-second glance at the water's edge, he saw Samir and Cooper running along the curved side of the cavern.

Body tingling from a sudden rush of adrenaline, he gulped a deep breath and swam with renewed effort. He had a chance of escaping death if he could outpace them to one of the small boats and drive it out of the grotto.

It seemed to take ages to reach the other side but to his amazement, when he reached the smallest of the boats, a 'cigarette' boat built for racing, Cooper and Samir were still running to catch up.

He sloshed aboard the boat. It was low and streamlined, like a floating sports car. The key was in the ignition. He flung off the mooring line and turned the key so hard he almost cut the fleshy pad of his thumb. The motor screamed and whined as he carved a deep swath of churning water on his way out of the grotto.

Bullets whished over his head and he ducked low as his stolen boat exploded from the mouth of the grotto into the open ocean.

Now what? He was free of the watery cavern, but he had no doubt Cooper would be right on his tail as soon as he got the other speedboat started.

Gas tank: full. He breathed a little easier. He scanned the horizon and turned the boat slightly westward. His quick thinking had gotten him into an even bigger pickle. Where to go now that he was in the open ocean, rapidly moving away from the Australian coast?

No sign of the sub. Can't chase it. Can't stop Cooper. His finger strayed to the GPS on the dashboard and tapped almost mindlessly. There was a preprogrammed destination in the menu list. He opened it. The map zoomed in on a small crooked piece of green way out in the middle of the ocean. An island.

Cooper's island.

Waves affected by the storm still whirling out there tossed his boat like butter in a churn, and any sane person would be heading in to safe harbor. But not him.

He had lives to save. Two of them, to be exact. His son, and the woman Bryce had married. Hopefully, they were still alive to be saved. Greg selected the destination and the GPS informed him in robotic tones of his next course correction.

Just as the sound of a motor behind him growled angrily. Cooper and Samir were following in the larger, but slightly slower powerboat. His own cigarette boat was of the type used for years to smuggle narcotics from the Caribbean into the States and designed for effortless speed. But the choppy waters weren't making it simple. It would be a race to the finish line.

"*Boom – Boom*" …Punctuated by gunfire.

Blake held Penny with one of his arms in a firm, protective grip as the hard-inflatable coast guard boat bounced through the water, blasting towards the island. Apparently, Agent Angelwing had a lead foot. But at least they would get there all the faster. That is, if the storm didn't swamp them first. They were literally heading right into the eye of the storm, against the advice of the coast guard and the navy to wait 24 hours for the storm to die down. A day could mean life or death to the two people stranded on that strip of land.

Life, Lord. Let it be life. Not death. If his brother was gone from this life and he wouldn't see him again until heaven – it would sap the joy from his existence. Suddenly Blake had an even bigger heaping amount of sympathy for Penny's loss of her fiancé.

She hid her face against him as sea-salt spray crashed over them, and he tried to shelter her against his side. He turned to look back at the larger coast guard boat following behind with the other agents. If it wasn't for the storm, they'd have one or two helicopters along too, Mark had told him.

"There it is!" Angel shouted over the noise of the wind and the sea. "Up ahead!"

Just a greenish shadow at first, the island quickly loomed ahead of them and seemed to expand before their eyes like a scene in a pop-up storybook. Markdown took the helm and guided them onto a sandy beach, barely scraping against some nasty rocks a few yards from the landing spot.

They'd clambered onto the sand before the other boat chugged in and dropped anchor.

"Look at this!" Angelwing screamed, her face gleaming with excitement. "We've got the right island!"

Huge letters formed of logs and rocks spelled the word "HELP" high on the beach, just outside the line of tropical foliage.

Bryce and Cara's handiwork.

Inside the shelter of the mountainside cave, Cara watched Bryce tinker with the black cube. He'd been carefully examining it and programming for a few hours. *I hope that thing works. It would be awesome to have a signal to help any rescuers find us.*

175

"All right. I think this will do it." Bryce selected a tab on the little screen that read "initiate program."

A loading bar appeared, then a box with four blank slots and a ticking time clock next to it. Above, it read "Please enter password, or self-destruct in 60 seconds." The 60 rapidly dwindled to 59, 58...

"AAAAH!" She screamed. "No!"

Bryce grunted in frustration. "Didn't see that coming!" He set down the cube and gripped both her arms in his hands. Stared into her face. "Cara. Focus. Help me think. What four characters would this guy have picked?"

He let go of her and closed his eyes. "It could easily be a random string of numbers and letters. Or not." He shook his head, eyes still closed. "This guy is arrogant. I doubt he'd care to choose something that wouldn't be hacked. Who'd hack it, way out here?" He opened his eyes.

His beautiful hazel eyes, always so full of love for her. In a few seconds, the life could be snuffed out of them if they didn't act.

"Should we run?" She suggested, jumping to her feet.

"No good. This thing probably holds a charge that could take out this whole mountain." The words came fast, rapid-fire. She could see his mind was whirring at top speed. Facial muscles tense. Eyes darting back and forth.

She tried to think, to put herself in Cooper's place. What would she have chosen if she were a crazed madman? *Hmm. That doesn't help.*

53, 52, 51...

"What does Cooper love most? Money, revenge, notoriety, fame...?" Cara talked it through out loud.

"Four letters!" Bryce started to key in 'fame', but stopped on the M. "We may have only one chance to answer this correctly." He erased the characters. "We've gotta make sure it's a really good guess."

48, 47, 46...

Silence held for a few more seconds. Then he grunted in frustration. "This would be easier if we knew him better."

39, 38, 37, 36, 35...

Cara felt panic pressing close on her chest. The cracked cavern walls seemed to be choking out the air around them. She reached for Bryce. "I'm so scared. Hold me!"

Her husband did one better. He quickly took her in his arms and kissed the side of her face, near her cheekbone. "I love you so much. You are everything to me." He pulled back a little bit and looked deep in her eyes. "Even *if* the time was short, I'm *so* glad God gave you to me as my wife."

Tears streamed down her face. "I love you too! *Still* glad I married you! I would do it again!" She kissed him desperately and he held her tight. Then they broke apart and Bryce picked up the cube again.

"Think!" She smacked her fist against her forehead.

Bryce nodded, his gaze on her face. They had to think, or they would die in... 24 seconds. 23. 22.

What would Cooper choose? What does he love? She asked herself again. *Wait.* She watched the contours of Bryce's face as emotions played across his expression, one after the other. *It's not a what – it's a who.*

She gasped. "Bryce! What was his brother's name?"

His eyes widened in comprehension. "Jack."

They nodded as one. His fingers trembled as he punched in the first three letters, then he stopped and reached for her hand, gripping it tightly. "I love you."

"I love you!" She echoed.

"Here's hoping..." he tapped the "K" key.

The clock froze. Then the numbers disappeared. They held their breath.

The loading bar filled all the way to the right side. Then more text appeared. "Program Initiated." The device began emitting the series of blips and beeps that spelled "SOS".

No signs of an explosion. Except from Bryce. "YEAH, BABY!" He yelled at the top of his lungs and swept her into his arms, spinning around in the center of the cave.

"Aaah!" She shrieked in relief, tears falling from her eyes and dropping onto Bryce's face below her. He blinked and stopped spinning, set her down. They collapsed to the sandy rock floor, taking deep breaths and wiping their faces.

Then he was kissing her – gladly, exuberantly. He leaned back and grinned. "Didn't know if I'd get to do that again."

She laughed and pulled him in for another kiss.

Thank you, God. I know you are with us.

Over the noise of the screaming wind and the rain pelting them like bullets, Blake, Penny, and the agents gathered on the beach heard a sound that didn't belong.

"BLIP-BLIP-BLIP – BEEEEP, BEEEEP, BEEEEP – BLIP-BLIP-BLIP"

S.O.S. Blake gasped. *It's an SOS. BRYCE! It has to be!*

Puzzlement and wonder splashed across the agents' faces along with mist from the ocean and sand-specked wind. "What is that?" Agent Goldenrod yelled.

Blake watched as Agents Markdown and Angelwing stiffened, straining to hear. Angelwing checked a handheld device gripped in her white-knuckled hands. "It seems to be coming from somewhere in the interior of the island. I'm picking up strong signals of biometric activity from the same place."

Then another noise cut through the clamor of the storm. An approaching small boat out at sea closed in, fought its way through the rocks, and landed onshore way down the beach, about two miles away from them. One lone figure hopped onto the sand and turned to face the sea, as if searching for something following.

Then a slightly larger speedboat appeared out on the horizon, but it circled around and disappeared on the other side of the island without making contact with them or the small boat.

"Northstar, Goldenrod, Spartan, go get that man and bring him here." Markdown pointed at the single person who had reached the beach. Those three set off at a quick jog to do as he'd asked while the rest of them took cover from the rain underneath the palm trees at the edge of the jungle.

While they were gone, Angelwing and Markdown laid out a plan of search and rescue, assigning positions and movement strategy to each member of the force aside from Blake and Penny, who were to stick with them.

The three agents returned with the stranger, and as they walked up, Blake felt a strange sensation in the pit of his stomach.

The man had graying sandy-brown hair, was about Blake's own height and build, but it was the face that snagged his attention.

High cheekbones, strong jawline, bold eyebrows over hazel eyes
and a mouth that looked capable of both kindness and firmness
– in short, he looked like an older version of his brother, Bryce.
Only slight differences in the nose and forehead, and deeper
lines around his eyes.

Dad.

Angelwing recoiled, grabbing Markdown's shoulder. She
recognized the man from the Agency hall-of-fame. "It's the
Gingerbread Man!"

Her husband's eyebrows rose and he took a closer look at the
newcomer.

Blake's tanned face was oddly white and pale, and he turned
slowly to face her. "What?!" He looked overwhelmed, as if he
might have a nervous breakdown. "He's *that* guy?!"

Penny slapped a hand over her mouth, eyes bulging like huge
blue marbles.

The man they were all staring at nodded. "And I assume you're
a taskforce from I.C.E. – recognized the insignia on your jackets
or I would have run instead of joined you." He pointed to Penny,
then Blake. "But these two obviously aren't-" He stopped,
scrutinizing Blake more closely. "... wait." He stepped closer.
"You remind me... of..."

"Dad."

The word that came out of Blake's mouth stunned them all into motionless silence.

Gregory Reynolds, for that was who he was, reacted first. "...I was going to say, you look like my wife, Dawn."

"...like Mom?" Blake still stared at the man like he was seeing a ghost from the past. Understandable.

"You have her eyes and nose." Greg took a step closer, stopped again. "You must be Blake."

"Oh. My. Word...." Penny looked about to faint. The other agents watched the drama unfolding with varying expressions of interest.

Angelwing tried to swallow but her throat was dry. *I can't believe I never made the connection. Bryce's father is the Gingerbread Man. Holy COW.* She hadn't known the Gingerbread Man's real name, and only glimpsed a grainy black-and-white photo of the man, which was ten years out of date.

Ten years. Gone. And his little boy, second-born child and dearly loved, had lost his chubby cheeks and grown into a strapping *man* with a lean athletic build. He'd been preparing to find Bryce, but the sudden appearance of Blake had bowled him over. He felt almost as weak and as full of mingling joy and the feeling of great responsibility as the day Blake was born.

And then Blake took a step towards him. He opened his arms and they met in the middle with a huge bear hug. Hot tears stung as they formed and fell.

He clutched his son in a tight embrace, still amazed at the feel of Blake's solid muscle and sheer size and that his little boy was a boy no more.

But we don't have any time to react to this. Cooper's out there.

He let go, wishing for all the world he didn't have to. "This is incredible, but we gotta move." He eyed the two agents who appeared to be in charge – a businesslike brunette and a tall blond man. *God, they're young. All of this team looks... too young! - I'm old, that's all.*

"Cooper Farnsworth was following me. That was his boat that ducked around to the backside of this island. Chances are he's already ashore. We have to find Bryce and ...Cara." In the heat of the moment, it took him a second to recall his new daughter-in-law's name.

"If they're still alive." One of the agents who'd greeted him broke in.

The in-charge brunette turned on the young man with a fierce glare in her big brown eyes. "If you make another remark like that, I *will* send you back to the boat to wait with Agent Toadspeckle!"

"Yes Ma'am." The agent subsided into subdued silence.

"We are operating under the assumption that they *are* alive, and the data is supporting that so far." She waved a handheld device in the other agent's face. "We'll follow this biometric signal until we reach them."

Greg nodded. *Impressive.*

She reached out a hand for him to shake. "Agent Angelwing, by the way." She waved to the other agent in charge. "My husband, Agent Markdown."

"Good to know." He thanked her. "Just call me Greg."

"Dad – this is Penny, my – uh – a good friend of mine." Blake touched the shoulder of the sweet-faced young woman with an extra helping of freckles on her cheeks, bringing her a little closer.

'Friend' indeed. It's obvious Blake cares about her more than that. He grinned as he took her hand. "Very pleased to meet you."

"It's amazing to meet you too, sir." Penny smiled, and her face went from pleasantly attractive to downright beautiful. Now he really wanted to see Bryce's girl. If she was anything like Blake's, his sons had been blessed indeed.

Speaking of Bryce... "All right, let's go!"

They all set off, crashing through the jungle, following the directional from Angelwing's screen.

Cooper ran along the hidden path, wet bracken thrashing him from all sides and branches whipping overhead from the storm winds. He'd told Samir to wait with the boat at the hidden lagoon. Once on the beach, he'd been surprised to find the remains of a crocodile skeleton, and then a collapsed hut a little closer inland. Signs of life.

That cursed couple – they were supposed to die in misery. I should have known! Why didn't I kill them when I had the chance?

For that matter, he should have suspected his quiet, unassuming foreman, Greg, long before now. But he'd missed the warning signs of the wolf in his herd of cattle, and gotten bitten in the hindquarters for it.

He headed for the cave, knowing it was the best shelter on the island if they were trying to ride out the storm. Drawing near to the mouth of the cave, he heard an SOS signal coming from his 378984 Audible Transmitter, instead of those great lion roars he'd chosen to terrify the island prisoners. Dismissing the question of how they'd disarmed the self-destruct sequence, he clambered inside. Laughter and soft voices reverberated from the back of the cave.

Anger stirred inside, like hot black pepper poured into boiling soup. He drew his handgun and cocked it, running forward until he saw them, lying on the cave floor. They looked up like startled deer at his approach.

"You're not dead." He ground out between his clenched teeth. "You're supposed to be dead." He raised the gun and aimed at Bryce's heart. "Let's fix that."

"Jack!" Cara shouted, surprising him into stillness.

"What?"

"The password. It was 'JACK'. You must have cared for him very much." Understanding rested in her eyes.

That was the last straw. To be pitied by this girl who knew nothing of his tortured soul and pain, lying awake nights in anguish because he hadn't kept his promise to his dying mother.

"Shut up!" He jerked the gun in her direction, which was a mistake. A hard, muscled form collided with his arm and then Bryce was endeavoring to wrench the weapon from his grasp.

Cara screamed as they struggled, writhing and punching and twisting. Bryce slammed his arm against the cave wall, trying to get him to drop the gun, and Cooper grunted in pain, but held fast to the pistol.

"You smell like a goat!" He sneered in the face of his younger enemy.

"Try not showering for about a week." Bryce reared his head back and banged his forehead into Cooper's skull. "*BAM!*" The world blackened near the edges and stars danced in the corners of his vision.

Julia Erickson

He fought back, pulling away and throwing a punch into Bryce's side. Bryce, unfazed, used the looser hold to crunch a powerful kick into Cooper's body, sending shooting pains up his whole left side.

And then out of nowhere, Cara shrieked like a wildcat and he felt a rock slam into the middle of his back, then another.

This wasn't playing out as he'd planned. Two against one – an older one – wouldn't lose.

Frantic, he took a chance and threw the gun into a dark corner of the cave. Bryce lunged after it and Cooper fled for the bright entrance.

"He's getting away!" Cara cried from behind as he made it outside. Bryce must have found the gun; two shots nearly ended Cooper as he fought his way through the jungle.

I've gotta get back to my boat. I have a nuclear missile to unleash. Forget these two for now. He knew when to retreat. But he would strike again when the moment was right – Bryce would yet pay for Jack's death. The rage still burned within him, and would not be quenched without vengeance.

CHAPTER TEN

Ransom and Revenge

Two shots echoed through the tropical trees and bushes, and the whole group of rescuers started running towards the spot they'd sounded from. Penny struggled to keep up, but without Blake's help she fell behind. He was staying close to his father's side, still looking like an awed little boy who couldn't believe his good fortune. After he'd introduced her, he seemed to promptly forget she existed.

That's okay. He just needs a little time – after all, it's been a decade since he last saw his dad!

He might need space, but she found herself missing Blake's attention – especially now, stumbling over tree roots. *When I get home, the first thing I'm going to do is mow the lawn! No more messy jungle around me!*

She tripped over a snagging vine and fell, slamming her palms into the damp earth. "Ugh." She wiped them against her pants, heaving herself up again to her feet. Penny couldn't see the bobbing heads of the agents in the underbrush anymore. She pushed ahead, looking for her companions, but all she saw was storm-tossed palm leaves and thick tangling vines.

"Hey!" She called. "Hey! Where are you guys?" *Yep. This "coming-along" thing was a bad idea. I don't have the skills to be a special agent!*

Then a man pushed out of the plants and looked up to see her. A big, brawny guy with slanty eyes and a huge hook nose, a dark shirt and tough canvas trousers stretched tight over his bulk.

Oh my gosh. Who is THIS? "Hello?"

He grinned. Not a pleasant sight. "A hostage!" He reached to grab her.

"I don't think so!" She squealed, trying to get away, but the undergrowth stopped her and he caught her arm.

Should have taken those self-defense classes at the police station!

"You are coming with me! Mistah Farnsworth will be most pleased!" His thick accent brought to mind pyramids and desert sands. Egyptian, perhaps.

"If he would just have let me use the gun, not grabbed for it, we wouldn't have gone on this wild goose chase or be in this mess at all, but NO, it had to be him to shoot Greg, not me..." He trailed off, muttering to himself. "So. We go see him. This pretty catch should make him happy!"

Not that I have much choice! Please God, help me!

Bryce stood next to his wife, staring out into the depths of the rain-soaked jungle below them. The sky still swirled with wind so strong it felt like the world was a top spinning out of control.

No sign of Cooper remained, nor a clue as to what direction he'd gone.

Okay. What's our next move? "Honey, we've got two choices. Chase blindly after Cooper, or climb higher to see where he has his boat. Either way, it's not likely we'll be able to get to whatever boat he brought, he's got a head start."

She looked back to the stormy landscape. "I feel like we should just be still." She shrugged. "I have no idea why – I've just got this sense that it's all been taken care of. We don't have to do this on our own strength."

Bryce's jaw dropped. "Well. Okay then." He tipped his face towards the sky. "Message received, God." He lifted a hand, palm up. "Thank you for whatever you're about to do."

And then, black-clad bodies emerged from the jungle just feet below them on the mountainside.

The group was made up of the Agency's top operatives, including Angelwing and Markdown, and his brother, Blake, walking alongside an older gentleman. They all started shouting at the sight of them. "Bryce! Cara!"

"Up here! We're here!" They jumped up and down and waved.

Bryce felt like he'd swallowed a quart of champagne, from the overwhelming tickle of joy that their lives had just been saved. *Thank you, God – thank you!*

The group swarmed up the hill and into the cave, out of the pouring rain. The first person to reach him was Blake – whom he was stunned to see here. Wordless, they met with a hard hug, pounding each other on the back – and then sobs wracking their frames.

He almost never cried, but this once, it was worth it.

And then things started happening all at once in a circus. Angelwing engulfed Cara in a tempestuous mama-bear hug, Markdown shook his hand, then Angelwing threw her arms around his neck, and the other agents pulled out a medical bag and started checking his and Cara's vital signs and gave them bottles of fresh water, which they gulped down.

Confusion reigned as everyone talked at once, but after they all expressed how glad they were that he and Cara were, in fact, alive, he finally managed to get the word across that Cooper had attacked them but left after Bryce got ahold of his gun.

The older gentleman had hung back during the whole exchange, but Bryce thought she'd seen watery tears rising in his eyes, and once he smiled kindly at Cara. *Hmm. Maybe she knows him from somewhere.*

Blake wiped his eyes and gestured to the older man. "Bryce, there's someone you need to meet."

Bryce nodded politely and stood, holding his hand out for a handshake, but when the older man clasped his hand, Bryce stared, then let go like his flesh was burned. "Oh my God."

"It's Dad!" Blake's voice cracked with emotion and excitement. "He's an intelligence agent too! Like you, even though you never told us. Looks like he didn't either."

I can't process this – my FATHER. After ten years, he just waltzes in here and expects us to simply – did he say AGENT?

His wife ran forward to stand next to him. But even her soothing presence couldn't stop his reaction.

"*You!*" Bryce felt his vocal cords shred a little on the inside. But it didn't even compare to the pain in his heart that the sight of his father inflicted on him.

The hubbub died down around them and everyone watched, like they were expecting a fistfight.

"Bryce." His father finally spoke, his voice sounding like an older, slightly deeper recording of him. Minus the intense rage. "I'm so glad you're all right."

"I am *not* all right!" he yelled, then caught himself and looked at all the other people watching him. Blake, shocked and a little hurt. Angelwing, sympathetic. Markdown, uncomfortable. Cara— he hated for her to see him like this. A little fear flickered in her eyes. *I never, ever want her to fear me.* It was that realization that finally calmed his upheaved emotions. "...But this is not the time to discuss it."

Cara placed a gentle hand on his tense, flexed shoulder. He relaxed under her touch and turned to look at her.

"It's okay." She whispered. The fear on her face was gone, replaced with tenderness. Compassion. Love.

He didn't reply, but reached up and covered her hand with one of his. *I truly don't deserve her.*

Angelwing hesitantly cleared her throat. "People, I know this is getting real, but we have work to do. Cooper Farnsworth has to be stopped from releasing his nuclear missile."

She's right. And time is short. "You know about the nuke?"

"Nuke?!" Blake seemed dumbfounded. "What nuke?"

"Yeah. We do." Markdown looked grim. "But not enough. Hopefully, he can tell us more." He indicated Bryce's father with a pointed finger.

"What?" *What could – he – possibly be able to tell us?*

Angelwing coughed. "You've heard of the Gingerbread Man?" Now she pointed to Greg. "He's him, and he's been working at Cooper's cattle station in the outback."

Bryce shifted on his feet. The news physically weakened him. "No. Way."

My father – the one they're always lauding as the best of the best? The man who performed so many daring feats and high-stakes stings that they don't even have them all on record? He'd held the Gingerbread Man as a hero to be imitated, dreamed of earning the same reputation.

But he's a fraud who forsook his family.

Cara didn't like the way Bryce's face had blanched. *I'm afraid he might faint!* "Do any of you have an energy bar or something?" She looked around at the other agents. "Our blood sugar levels are rock-bottom."

A female agent with wild curly hair slipped several of them out of a bag and handed them to her. She gave two to Bryce and thanked the curly-headed agent with a smile as Markdown started to bring them all up to date. "The nuclear-equipped submarine was sighted leaving Cooper's property and heading out to sea at 0800 hours…"

Cara tried to listen but almost before she realized it, she nearly slipped out of consciousness and was falling to the floor in a faint herself.

Bryce noticed and darted towards her, but it was Blake who caught her before that could happen and helped her sit on a smooth rock along the side of the cave.

She opened her eyes wide and looked at her brother-in-law. "Thank you!"

"Hey, no prob." He shrugged it off and sat next to her. Bryce and the others resumed their briefing once they realized she was all right.

"I still haven't heard why *you* showed up with the rescue team. I think you and I are the only non-agents here." She smiled, trying to lighten the atmosphere.

Blake half-smiled. "Yeah, you and me and Penny-" He stopped talking and scanned the room. Jumped up. "Where's Penny?!"

"Penny! What are you talking about? She came too?" Shock colored her voice and made it embarrassingly squeaky.

Everyone halted, then started talking at once. "Who saw her last? Where could she be? Penny!?"

A piercing whistle from Markdown stopped the noise. "Northstar, Spartan, you guys start looking for her. Move out in concentric circles and see if you can figure out where she got separated from us." He picked up one of the supply bags and hefted it onto his shoulder. "We'll all retrace our steps and head back to the boat, maybe she returned there."

Cooper was livid with rage when he found his power speedboat empty, with no sign of his sidekick Samir. *It's so hard to find good help these days! I thought I could at least count on him!*

He felt a moment's dread. *Is he a turncoat like Greg?*

But then Samir came thundering out of the tropical trees, dragging a girl behind him. She was kicking and struggling against him. *What a little spitfire. But how-?*

"Explain this!" Cooper ordered.

Samir looked up. "Ah! Yes, Sah. I found this hostage –"

"But in the process, you left the boat! I specifically told ya to wait here!"

Samir had the decency to look downcast. He nodded. Then brightened. "But now we've got her." He gave the girl's arm a shake as if she were a rag doll. She cried out, but sounded more mad than hurt.

Plucky little thing. "Get her onboahd." He climbed up the boat ladder ahead of them and pulled out his smartphone. *This could turn out to be very advantageous indeed.* "Stow her below deck and head back to the station."

He had a phone call to make. He dialed the number for the "International Federal Publishing house" – what he knew to be the front for whatever secret government operation Bryce Reynolds worked for – the same place he'd sent the warning note about the Black Swan.

While he waited for the call to go through, he checked on his precious submarine. *Yes. She's still on course.*

At the boat, a huge surprise was waiting for them. *Another* boat – one from the Agency. Bryce noticed a cocoa-skinned man standing in the bow, who lifted a hand in greeting. *It's Monty! What's he doing here?* Unfortunately, there was no sign of

Penny. Angelwing radioed Northstar and Spartan, but they hadn't found any signs of her either. They were heading back to the beach to meet up.

The other agents recognized their boss as they boarded the boat and greeted him in turn.

Montrose nodded to Angelwing and Markdown and then gripped Bryce's hand in a tight handshake, eyes shining. "Agent Ashburn – you don't know how glad I am to see you still breathing."

He laughed, shaking Monty's hand with vigor. "It's good to see you too, boss." He'd missed the dry humor in Monty's voice. Hearing it again gave him confidence that they'd see out this mission just like the rest of them.

Montrose and Cara shared a gentle hug and then Monty turned to... his father. "With you, however, I have a bone to pick."

Greg Reynolds looked gray and tired, sighing. "I know-"

"You deliberately ignored orders to join the extraction team in Canberra and we got a great satellite view of you jeopardizing your life with a hazardous boat chase on the way here. What were you thinking, man?"

What in the world? Monty was giving my father orders? "HOLD ON a second!" Everyone turned to look at him at the sound of his shout.

"Are you telling me you-" he pointed at Montrose, "-know *him*-" he pointed at his father- "And didn't tell ME?" He finally pointed at himself.

A look of – *is it guilt?* – splashed across the faces of both his father and Monty. "Bryce, I'm sorry. But yes – your father and I have been sporadically in contact for the past ten years." Montrose's tone was apologetic, but firm. "In fact, one of the reasons I sought you out after the academy was that you were his son, and I was hoping you were of the same caliber as your father. Who is, I might add, an excellent spy."

MIND. BLOWN. Everything and everyone he had always known to be rock-solid had just shattered into a million shards like a smashed mirror. The reflection he'd believed in was gone – replaced by reality.

Reeling from the shock, he stumbled back a step into his wife, who caught and held him with an arm around his back.

"I had a good reason for going dark, son-" His father started to talk, but Bryce cut him off. "-Stop. Just... stop." He gulped a breath into his empty lungs. "For one thing, I can't handle this right now, for another, we are running out of time to stop Cooper's nuclear strike."

"And we still have to find Penny!" Cara inserted, "We can't leave without her!"

Before anyone else could speak, Montrose's private phone rang shrilly from his jacket pocket. He answered it, then his face went ashen. "Put him on." He hit the speaker button.

Cooper Farnsworth's voice buzzed from the phone, sounding as if he was having to shout over the hum of a motor. "G'day mates. I've got a little friend here with me – she's got the prettiest red hair."

"-Let *go* of me!" Penny's voice.

Cara looked ready to throw up.

"Let her go, Cooper." Bryce injected some of his fury into his tone.

"Ah. So Mistah Montrose put me on speakah. Hello, mates! Here's how it's gonna work." Cooper's voice had taken on almost a chipper, lilting tone. But it was off-key, giving the listeners a sense that the person using it must be mentally imbalanced. "We're all going back to my place for a little – pahty. Yeah. And here's what you're gonna do – hand over Bryce Reynolds, or I'll kill the girl. Without a second thought. Is that cleah?"

Cara felt as if her world had turned completely inside out. She and Bryce had just been saved, but now her best and truest girlfriend was in mortal danger. *And the only solution is to give up my husband?! What if we lose both of them?!*

"Hold on." Mr. Montrose hit the silencing button, and everyone started forcefully talking at once.

"We can't do that!"-"She's not an asset!"-"What are you talking about?"-"We can't just give him Bryce!"

"QUIET!" Montrose brought the chaos to a halt.

"I'll do it." Bryce offered, determination on his face.

Cara let out a single hiccuping sob, covering her mouth. *NO! But – Oh, he's so amazing – Oh God, what do we do?*

"You most certainly will not." Montrose snapped. "Not without a plan." He punched the button to turn on the volume once more. "What are your terms?"

"You want specifics, ay? Well then. I'll give you until seven o'clock to bring Bryce Reynolds to the back gate of my cattle station. Then you'll get the redhead."

A muffled shout from Penny echoed in the background. "Don't do it Bryce- Mmmphf!" She was suddenly silenced.

"If you don't show, the girl dies. Slowly. And he had bettah be alone! No heroics!" Cooper threatened.

"Then who are you planning to hand your hostage off to, Mr. Farnsworth?!" Monty demanded.

"Oh, well then, you can bring a friend. ONE friend. He can collect the hostage. Fair dinkum? See ya latah." He hung up.

Just then, Agents Northstar and Spartan climbed aboard. "We couldn't find Miss Penny-"

"Cooper has her!" Cara shrieked. *My best friend is in the hands of a murdering madman!*

"Everyone – into the cabin. We'll discuss this inside." Montrose directed. "Agent Wildcat, man the helm and set a course for Cooper Farnsworth's property on the coast of Australia. We don't have much time. Tell Agent Toadspeckle to follow behind in the other boat."

Cara felt herself begin to hyperventilate as they marched into a room with a table in the center. Along the walls, artillery weapons and all sorts of spy gear rested in compartments organized with utmost efficiency. Bryce squeezed her hand, then addressed the group. "I have to do it, there's no other option! We don't have time to replicate a face mask for a stand-in and Cooper's no fool. It's gotta be me."

Mr. Montrose frowned, obviously mulling it over. He turned to Bryce's father. "Greg, do you have a better option? You know the ranch better than anyone else."

The engine thrummed to life and they felt the Agency boat pull away from the island into the open water.

"I think we can get in to the ranch house. Cooper has a secured room in the basement, where he keeps his secrets."

Mr. Montrose nodded as if in comprehension. "The safe room. You described that in your reports."

"Yes – all his most priceless valuables are there, locked in a safe, as well as incriminating files and a separate computer. I'll bet that's where he's got the kill switch for the nuke."

Cara had seen Bryce's expression darkening like storm clouds as his father spoke, and suddenly, the thunder unleased. "*How* do we know we can trust *him*?!" He demanded, glaring at his father.

"Look." Blake caught all their attention by stepping in between the two men. "We have a situation here. I'm no agent, even though the both of you are, as well as all these guys." Blake looked at the team of agents standing behind Mr. Montrose. "-but even I can see we need to buckle down, stuff our personal grievances for now, and form a truce so we can tackle this problem head-on. We can do it if we just *work together*."

A brief silence enfolded them as Blake's impassioned words sank in.

"He's right." Montrose declared. "Bryce, Greg, get your heads in the game. Are you with me?"

Greg Reynolds nodded soberly. Bryce turned to the wall for a moment, and Cara could see his lips moving silently. Then he swiveled back around, face cleared. "Yes."

The Bryce she knew was back, looking remarkably like he had just before they stormed the castle back in Munich, on their last mission. Resolve shone in his eyes. "I'm here to serve my country."

Relief flooded her, staring at him – a picture of a hero. *My hero.*

"Good. Speaking of our country, do we have a target yet?" Montrose searched for an answer in the faces of his agents.

"We're estimating somewhere along the west coast of the states, but nothing specific yet." Agent Markdown supplied the facts.

"Cooper told us he was going to hit America. That's all we know." Bryce stated. "I think he said it would be 'blown to bits'!"

They all braced themselves as the boat hit a patch of particularly rough waters. The hurricane winds had died down, but it was still ugly out there.

"Cooper's barely given us enough time to get to his property." Greg looked worried. "But I think I know what we have to do..."

Cooper let Samir handle the girl after they landed at the shoreline of his property. They drove one of the trucks for a few miles and then entered the back gate. Cooper instantly called on the intercom for two men to guard it with machine guns. He, Samir, and the irritated hostage then headed back to the house – but when they arrived, to his surprise, his wife was standing on the veranda watching them.

Horror carved her face as she caught sight of Penny, grimy and with her hands tied together behind her back with a short length of rope. "Cooper! What's going on?!" She spread her hands and fingers, ready to receive any explanation.

"Put her in the bunkhouse." He murmured in Samir's ear. He left the captive and Samir and stalked to his wife's side. "You weren't meant to see this, my deah." He grabbed her elbow. "It would have been bettah that way."

Veronica meekly submitted as he led her through the house and into the master bedroom. "What are you doing?" Her pleas for information were getting on his nerves.

"What I must do. It's none of your concern. Trust me – just forget you ever saw anything."

"But what are you going to do to her-?"

"-Shut up, woman!" He lost his temper. "Stay here!" He marched out the door. The old vintage door had a keyhole and an intricately shaped iron handle. He rummaged in a drawer of the hall table and came up with a padlock, and snapped it over the handle, locking his wife in from the outside.

Muffled whimperings came drifting through the door. *I'm not going to stop now just because some Sheila doesn't approve of my actions. I've gone too far.*

He stomped to the jackaroos' bunkhouse to ensure that Samir had safely stowed their hostage and to gather his men and assign them to their posts for the company he was expecting. To his satisfaction, Penny was tossed in a corner of the second floor of the bunkhouse. He left five of his burliest jackaroos guarding the building and sent out a squad to patrol the fenceline – reserving his most loyal men to hunker down outside the safe room in the basement.

The briefcase should be safer in there than on my person. I don't want anyone around to screw things up. When he met Bryce Reynolds again, nothing would go wrong. Even if the agent somehow managed to get the better of him again, as had happened back in the cave, the metal briefcase holding the brains that communicated remotely with the nuclear missile would be untouchable – locked in the safe room, inside the wall safe.

The last step he took was to grab a tablet, connected to his high-speed wifi, so he could have a bird's-eye view of the havoc he was about to wreak on the USA. Revenge would be all the sweeter watching the expression on Bryce Reynolds' face when he saw a gigantic chunk of his homeland falling into the sea.

The Agency boat and the coast guard boat following it avoided the underground grotto harbor. Greg thought Cooper would be expecting them to come in there. Instead, he directed them farther down the coast to an inlet without any sharp cliffs where the land sloped down to the sea. Evening was closing in, though the overcast sky made it difficult to guess the hour. At least the rain that had followed them over from the island ended a few miles back and the swollen skies held back from unleashing the water droplets.

Cooper's massive property was three thousand, six-hundred square miles, and the small compound around the ranch house was fenced with a spiked concrete wall all the way around. It would be tricky to creep in unseen, but their taskforce could do it if they chose an unexpected place to attack.

Greg looked at the people around him. All seemed fit enough except for Bryce and Cara, who were weakened from their stint on the deserted island. If he had a choice, he would have dropped them off at an Agency safe house instead of dragging them along on the raid. But there had been no place to do so, and they needed Bryce to 'exchange' for Penny.

"Okay people, here's what we've got going in." Angelwing swiped and zoomed quickly on her tablet, checking satellite and infrared images. "Looks like there are about twenty unfriendlies along the perimeter of the compound. Two at the back gate, two moving towards it. A whole cluster of them is at this spot in the main house-" she showed them a blobby mass of orange bodies in the otherwise purple shades of the structure – "-and I'm guessing that's the safe room."

Greg confirmed her statement with a nod. "Let me." He took the tablet from Angel's hands and examined the readouts himself. "Here we've got about five or six guys guarding... the bunkhouse? Why would they do that? Unless that's where they've got Penny." He zoomed in a little more. "Yes. There's a small orange dot on the second floor." He zoomed to max, and they could see a vague orange outline of Penny, crouching in the corner with her hands behind her back and head bowed.

Cara gasped at the sight. Blake looked like wanted to punch something – hard.

"Come on, people. We know what we're all doing. Let's get this show on the road." Markdown chopped the air with his hand in a signal to move out.

CHAPTER ELEVEN

Raid on the Ranch

Bryce was glad he and Cara had at least had a chance to shower and eat while on the Agency boat. They'd also shot him up with some adrenaline injections and a fluids IV drip. He felt like a human again in a fresh black jumpsuit, but he knew he wasn't at full strength after the starvation diet.

Markdown jogged alongside him as they moved into position, heading for the back gate. They were wired, with audio transmitting back and forth between them and the other two teams. His father, Monty, and the other agents were entering at a quiet point along the east wall. Blake and Angelwing would split from the group once they gained access to the compound and head for the bunkhouse.

Bryce and Markdown would have a standoff with Cooper at the back gate and stall as long as possible. Meanwhile, their strongest force would infiltrate the safe room in the basement.

He looked over at his friend – perhaps his closest friend, aside from Cara. Mark looked back. "Ready for this, man?"

"I know I am. But I'm concerned about you." Markdown moved easily, lightly running with the lithe grace of a panther. "Are you physically up for it? Is your head in the right place?"

"My head's fine. As for the rest of me – I've gotta be." *No other choice.*

The back gate loomed in the distance, and they slowed to a walk. Heartbeat thumping in his ears, Bryce took in the sight. The spiked concrete wall stretched across the flat land like a toothy jaw. The gate in the center waited to swallow them whole. Two men stood at the ready, all in khaki gear with Thompson M1921 Sub-machine guns held at the ready. They trained the guns on them as they approached.

Markdown discreetly tossed a little circular disk behind him, leaving it blinking faintly in the dust.

The gates swung open and there stood Cooper and a huge, swarthy man with hooded eyes. Must be Samir, from his father's description of the henchman.

The two guards moved forward and frisked them, checking for weapons and finding none. They resumed their posts.

"G'day, Mates." Cooper greeted them genially, his Aussie twang as present as ever. But menace lurked in his cold eyes. His mouth twisted in a contemptuous sneer. "Glad you could make it."

"Where's Penny?" Bryce couldn't take any more of the 'pleasantries' – even though he knew they needed to draw out the time.

"Ah, Penny! So that's the name of the little spitfire." Cooper chuckled, the lines in his weathered face deepening in amusement.

Samir stopped glaring and grinned, then resumed his fierce stare.

"She was less than cooperative, I must say." Cooper scratched his chin. "Gave us quite a bit o' trouble on the trip here. Neahly lost her over the side o' the boat. We were forced to restrain her."

"If you laid one finger on her..." Bryce clenched a fist low, next to his side.

"Rest assured, the worst that's wrong with Miss Penny is some dust on her little freckled nose."

Cooper pulled out a tablet and gazed at the screen. "Right-o. Everything's in ohdah." He looked up at the two of them. "Time you came with me, *Bryce.*" He infused Bryce's name with poison on the way out of his mouth.

Yikes. This guy really hates me.

"Not so fast." Markdown took a wider stance. "You promised a trade. Penny for Bryce."

"Hah!" Cooper barked out a dry laugh. "You'll get the girl when I say so. You wait here, misteh."

Samir stepped forward and wrapped a long hand around his bicep, half dragging him over to Cooper. Samir's own muscles stood out in sharp relief underneath his tight t-shirt. The men moved back inside the compound, leaving Markdown at the open gate with the other two guards.

He risked a glance over his shoulder. Markdown stood with his arms crossed, chin high, slightly-too-long hair brushed by the breeze. He nodded reassuringly at Bryce, though his eyebrows were tensed in unease.

They had suspected that Penny wouldn't be given up so easily, but to have it happen was disappointing.

"I thought you were a man of your word, Cooper." Bryce taunted, hoping to provoke a reaction and slow Cooper down.

Cooper whirled in his tracks. "Oh, I am. And to prove it, just watch what I'm gonna do to your country – just like I said I would. The whole state of California will pay for what you did to my brothah."

Not if we can call off your missile first!

A lime-green lizard skittered away from his foot, barely escaping being crushed against the red dirt. Blake followed the others up the slope. Just a thin line of trees separated them from the compound.

Angelwing checked the infrared again. "No guards at this point." She kept her mellow voice to a soft whisper. "Let's move."

They followed her, single file, crouching low and moving as silently as possible. Agent Spartan pulled a huge black weapon out of his knapsack and pulled the trigger. A length of cord sailed over the spiked wall with a sharp anchor on the other end that caught and held with a scratchy thud.

One-by-one, the agents climbed up and over the wall, the nimblest of the group going first. Then they hoisted up his father, then Cara, then finally Mr. Montrose, bringing up the rear. Each had to take the utmost care not to step on the sharpened spikes of dark metal poking out from the top of the concrete wall as they made it over.

Once inside, the group split. He and Angelwing snuck their way towards the bunkhouse while the rest of them crept towards Cooper's dwelling.

Blake followed Angelwing's movements, stopping when she stopped, sprinting when she sprinted. She pressed herself against the wall of the bunkhouse and he did likewise. She checked the infrared one last time. "On my count." She whispered, then mouthed "Three – two – one –" She kicked the door open.

The scent of unwashed bedsheets and musky cologne assailed them as the door flew open. Five men jumped up in surprise from their bunks, but before two of them could use the rifles in their hands for detrimental purposes, they had been silenced by two bullets fired from the semi-automatic pistol in Angelwing's grip. The gun had a silencer so as not to alert the other people in the compound around them.

Blake covered the two closest guards at gunpoint from the .357 IMI Desert Eagle pistol they'd given him from the Agency boat arsenal, while Angelwing pointed hers at the last fellow. "Up the stairs, you. And make it snappy."

The man did as she said and she followed him up the creaking board steps. "Untie her." Angel's voice ordered. "And remove that gag!"

Then a sound that thrilled him down to his toes. "Angelwing!" Penny's voice.

One of the two men he was watching shifted, and he tilted the gun's barrel slightly more toward him. "Don't even think about it." The hardness in his own tone surprised him. He'd be more at ease charming this guy into buying a house from him, but here he was – holding people at gunpoint!

Is this what Bryce does all the time?

The steps creaked again under the tread of the third man, who was followed by Angelwing and Penny. Penny's arms and face were smudged with dirt and her hair tangled, but her eyes shone when she caught sight of his face. "Blake!"

"Hey gorgeous." He wanted to run to her, but instead kept his gun trained on the two men.

Angelwing spoke into the air, but Blake knew the words were meant for Markdown and the mic in Angel's ear would pick them up. "We've got her." She listened for a second, then nodded. "Take this gun and point it at him." Angelwing pulled another pistol off her hip and handed it to Penny, jerking her chin at the third man.

"Oh my gosh." Penny took the gun and did as instructed as Angelwing made short work of zip-tying the man's hands together behind his back and fastening him to the bedpost of the solid wooden bunk-bed. She did the same to the other two and then Blake was free to lower his weapon.

The first thing he did was crush Penny to his chest in a hug. "You're okay?!" He rested his cheek on top of her head.

She clung to him, shaking. "I'm okay. I'm okay!" She snuggled tight against him. "Now that you're here – more than okay."

Angelwing snorted behind her. "You two are adorable."

Penny jerked her head up. "Bryce and Cara?! Are they okay? I heard Bryce's voice on the phone during the ransom call-"

"We got them off the island – but I'm not sure where they are now. Cara is with the other agents; Bryce went to go meet Cooper-"

"Time to go." Angel peeked out the window in the direction of the ranch house. "Things are about to get hot-n'-heavy."

Markdown kept his back turned to the sandy path behind him – along which he'd dropped a micro-bomb. Once Angelwing relayed that they had Penny, he bit down on the button of the remote stuck to one of his molars.

"KA-BLOOEY" A puff of dust and smoke shot up from the microbomb's explosion, leaving a small crater behind it. The guards jerked in shock and stared towards the spot. The distraction gave him just enough time to take out one of the men's guns with a flying kick. He caught it before it hit the ground and sent about five bullets into the other guard before he could fire on Markdown. The man whose gun he'd used lunged for him but was too slow to avoid the mighty whack of the gun barrel Markdown sent in a spinning move into the man's jaw.

He left them there, lying unconscious on the ground, as he sprinted for the main house. He took up a defensive position at the south corner, ready for any of the guards along the walls who might hear the commotion and come running. He checked his own infrared screen. Yep. Here they came. Orange figures were bolting across the indigo blue screen in his direction.

Someone had to make the exit path clear for the others, and the task had fallen to him. Once there were no more unfriendlies, he could go after Bryce, who had been marched off with Cooper.

I won't let him down.

Cara gasped for breath. The running and climbing had taken a toll on her weakened body, even with lots of help from the other agents. She was rethinking her insistence that she not be left behind at the boat with Agent Toadspeckle. Sitting down sounded awfully good right now.

But now they were inside the ranch house, having slipped through the window in Greg Reynold's bedroom. It was on a shaded side of the house amid some trees and bushes and faced away from the other buildings. But once they were in, shots rang out from what sounded like the back gates and they heard shouts from the guards inside the house and running feet.

Agent Northstar opened the bedroom door and leaped out, gun blazing. The hallway erupted into a war zone. Greg Reynolds kept her behind him, using himself as a human shield. They and Agent Spartan and Mr. Montrose edged their way out of the room under the cover of the gunfire from the rest of the agents and raced towards the safe room.

When they descended into the basement, all hell broke loose and they were met by a cloud of bullets. They ducked for cover, but not before Cara felt what seemed like a punch on the very edge of her waist. She glanced down to see torn fabric where a bullet had scraped by her bulletproof vest. Greg slammed her behind him and he and Agent Spartan fired into the darkness. The return fire ceased, and Greg leaned around the door frame to look. "Clear!" He dragged her behind him as he dodged through the doorway. Cara nearly tripped over – the prostrate form of Mr. Montrose!

"Monty!" She gasped. The man was lying on the ground, hand over his gut. He pulled a bullet out of his Kevlar vest and looked up at her. "Go. GO!" He gasped, short of breath from the bullet's impact. "I'll be fine!" She obeyed, though hating to leave him there. She crawled through the black basement, thinking that at any moment a bullet could come zinging out of the dark. But she made it to the other end, where Agent Spartan and Greg Reynolds crouched near a steel door. The safe room.

Agent Spartan had slapped a blinking metal rectangle over the door's keypad and Cara looked over his shoulder to see it decode the password, which was a random string of numbers. Not "JACK" this time.

Spartan reached for the door handle but let out a cry and collapsed, unconscious. Cara shrieked. Greg checked the pulse at the agent's throat. "Alive." He examined the door handle. "Must be electrified. He's in shock." He looked around in the dark basement. "Find something rubber."

Shelves of tools and miscellaneous basement junk lined the walls, and Cara frantically searched for something they could grip the door handle with. She could hear Greg doing the same. Then she caught a break —finding a ripped, dirty rubber disposable glove in a cardboard box stuffed with cleaning rags. "Here!"

"Good girl." He took the glove from her and opened the door, looked inside. Cara peeked around too. A curvy woman with platinum blonde hair stood in front of a glass case full of jewelry made with precious gems, completely ignoring the display cases of rare Australian artifacts and the safe door on the back wall. She clutched a small pearl-handled .22 handgun.

Then the woman lifted her head – Greg leapt out of sight just as she looked at them, so the woman saw only Cara. She raised the gun and stared at her. "And who are you?!" She inquired, abandoning her efforts to get at the gems.

Cara gulped, resisting the urge to look at Greg and give away his presence. "I'm – uh... Cara Reynolds. You must be Mrs. Farnsworth?"

The woman nodded. "Whatever are you doing here?!"

Distraction. I've got to get her attention so Greg can get to that safe! Cara stepped tentatively inside the safe room. "It's a crazy story, actually..."

Bryce's arm was going numb in the none-too-gentle grasp of Samir the Egyptian Brute. They followed Cooper's proud, marching footsteps across the compound. Cooper seemed like he was having a grand old time and everything was going his way, strutting along like a dictator on parade. "Right this way, mates, and we can watch the fireworks."

They were heading towards a flat square wooden platform on a small rise. A tripod with a telescope atop it perched on one corner, aimed at the sky.

"This is what I like to call my 'observatory'." Cooper announced, with a wide sweep of his free hand. The other clutched his tablet. "So it's only right and fitting, you see, that we stand here to *observe* the destruction." The man laughed like a giddy child on a carousel ride, and then it trailed off in an unsettling giggle. His eyes were glazed.

He's losing it. Bryce realized. *He's on the brink of a mental breakdown!* Even Samir looked a bit distressed, and screwed up his mouth in nervousness.

"Watch the screen." Cooper commanded them. Bryce did as the man said and kept his eyes on an aerial view of what looked like a dam.

"This is where the missile will strike." Cooper let loose with another spine-tingling giggle. "And because it's along the fault line, the entire state of California will fall off and crumble into the ocean." He glared at Bryce. "A fitting recompensation for the murder of my poor, innocent brother."

"He was trying to kill me when I shot him." Bryce reminded him. "So you say! Nobody's here to tell his side of the story. Jack's dea-hea-heaaad!" Cooper broke down and sobbed, wiping his eyes.

Now Samir looked downright uncomfortable. "Sah – please Sah, don't cry-"

"Don't you dare tell me what to do!" Cooper snapped, but at least he stopped the heaving sobs. Then he pulled out his phone. "Release the vengeance of the Black Swan!" He roared, his face purpling. Then he eagerly stared at the screen. "See! She's launched!" He started to turn it towards Bryce.

NO! No, no, no.... Panic cracked his calm façade and he could feel himself trembling.

Just then, the sound of machine-gunfire rattled out from the back gate. A few seconds later, shots echoed from inside the ranch house.

"What was that?!" Cooper shrieked. "No, Samir, you stay with this murderer, I will go see for myself."

Cooper hopped down off the platform. He threw one last "Stay!" over his shoulder as he walked off to investigate the noise, which continued unabated.

Bryce and Samir looked at each other. The Egyptian blinked. "I don't like this." He grumbled. He let go of Bryce and brought his gun up to aim at Bryce's heart. "Maybe I should just kill you now and then take out Cooper. He has a great fortune I could steal."

"Wow, aren't you a peach of an assistant!" Bryce took a step back. "But if you did that, you'd be making a big mistake."

Any second now, I'm about to be killed, and that missile will hit California. Please, God, do something!

"Hmmm." Samir seemed to be weighing his options. "Nah, it sounds like a good plan to me." His finger tightened on the trigger, but that was the last thing he ever did. Shots rang out and suddenly the man was face-down on the ground, a crimson stain spreading underneath him. He'd knocked the telescope down with him and shattered glass from the lens was sprinkled across the growing pool of blood.

Markdown leaped out from behind the nearest Acacia tree and ran to his side. "I've got Bryce!" he shouted into the air, no doubt for the benefit of those listening in on his wire.

"Thanks, Man!" His heart was racing from the close call. "Talk about an answer to prayer!"

"Just returning the favor." They shared a quick look, both remembering the last time he had saved Markdown's life. Barely. "Where's Cooper?!" Mark asked, scanning the compound. The madman had vanished – not such a tough thing to do with brush and trees scattered everywhere inside the concrete fence. Even the tops of the buildings were partially obscured from view.

"I think he's headed towards the house – and he's released the missile!"

" – so after your husband left us on the beach, Bryce and I had to figure out what to do. We had no food, and no fresh water, all we had were our wits and our love for each other." Greg watched as Cara continued the tale she'd been spinning to the woman for the past few seconds.

Cara, clever girl, had moved ever so slightly around the table in the center of the safe room until Veronica's back was turned to him, waiting outside the doorway in the dark basement. He silently padded inside the bright steel-walled room and took three noiseless steps until he was standing at the wall safe.

Mrs. Farnsworth still stood slack-jawed, listening to Cara's amazing story. The girl told it well, with fire and passion in her eyes and expressive hand movements that helped keep the woman's attention centered on her.

"The next morning, we ripped up my cotton cardigan and used it to soak up fresh water from the dew on the grass…"

He studied the safe. It had been *ages* since he had done any safe-cracking. He leaned close to the cold metal and listened as he turned the dial. The tumblers clicked gently into place, one-by-one, as Cara described the different things she and Bryce had tried to find food. When she got to the crocodile attack, even he had a hard time believing her. But Veronica Farnsworth seemed mesmerized, and the gun drooped lower and lower in her hand until it was aimed not at Cara, but the floor.

The last tumbler fell, and the safe swung open. Inside sat a silver metal briefcase. He opened it to discover a black screen that lit to life – and on the bottom half, a keyboard and the proverbial 'big red button'. *What do you know – it's even red.* The brains that remotely controlled the TOMAHAWK X12 missile. But a feeling like lead settled inside him when he realized the missile was airborne. It had already released from the submarine! What was worse, when he began to input the divert path order, he realized the system was encrypted.

He swore under his breath. Then stopped. *Sorry, Lord. But please — God in heaven, help me turn this thing around in time!* He knew he could decrypt it, but it would take time — that they *didn't* have. But he had no choice but to try.

"...Then the hurricane moved in, and we had to abandon the hut! I think it must have gotten knocked over from the storm..." Cara bravely continued her narrative behind him.

Come on. Come on. He silently coaxed his brain to work faster.

Then let out a shout of triumph as he broke the encryption on only his *second* attempt, nothing short of a miracle, and instantly slammed the button. "Hah!"

That startled Veronica Farnsworth, who whirled around and aimed the gun at him. "Greg! What are you doing?!" She wobbled unsteadily on her high heels.

"Mrs. Farnsworth, that's my father-in-law. He's stopping a terrible tragedy from happening. Your husband has been planning a terrorist attack on America." Cara's voice was steady and firm, each word crisply enunciated.

The woman's face crumpled, her mouth curving down and lines deepening around her black-rimmed eyes. "Oh no! I thought – I thought he was a good man. Not very warm or cuddly, but I trusted him!" She started crying. "But today he showed up with that poor girl tied up and then locked me in my room and I was so scared – I had to crawl out the bathroom window and get in through the kitchen-" She hiccupped. "I thought if I could just take my jewels I could-" She'd been waving the gun wildly as she spoke, but in an instant, Cara grabbed her wrist and snapped it down on her thigh, popping the weapon from Veronica's grasp.

What a girl! Bryce has found himself a treasure. Steady under pressure, quick-thinking, intelligent – and beautiful to boot!

Veronica shrank like a wilting violet as the gun went skittering across the floor and Cara snatched it up. "I wasn't going to shoot anyone! That was for my own protection!" Trickles of salty tears and black mascara stained her cheeks.

"Just making sure no accidents happen!" Cara shoved the gun into the pocket of her black jumpsuit.

Greg turned from the sorry sight back to the computer screen. "LAUNCH ABORTED" flashed across the top. Somewhere in the middle of the ocean, the missile had died and plopped into the water, probably to sink to the ocean floor among the shipwrecks of the deep.

He took a huge breath and blew it out. *Thank you, Lord!* "The nuke's been neutralized." He closed the briefcase.

"Greg, you're-" Veronica sniffed. "You're not a ranch foreman?!"

"Afraid not, ma'am." He blinked. "Only a special agent."

The darkness of evening cloaked the land. Penny hurried behind Angelwing, hand-in-hand with Blake as they hustled towards the ranch house. She couldn't begin to describe the relief she'd felt when the terror of being a tied-up captive gave way to the blessed joy of being rescued. And by a kick-butt secret agent and a knight in shining armor, no less.

Angel stopped suddenly, listening. A grin cracked her face. "We've got Bryce."

She and Blake reacted with hushed exclamations of relief. "Oh, good!" "Awesome!"

Thank you Lord! Now if we can just get everyone out of here safely... They resumed their trek to the main house.

"When we have time," Blake leaned closer to speak softly, "We have a lot to talk about."

She could feel a huge smile opening across her face. "I think you're right." Butterflies performed an excited dance of anticipation inside her.

His eyes crinkled at the corners and he winked at her.

It wasn't exactly a short walk in from the bunkhouse, more like two miles. Thankfully, they hadn't come across any more guards. Angel said she suspected Markdown had taken them out from the sounds over her earpiece.

They'd reached the veranda when around the corner came the one and only Cooper Farnsworth, muttering to himself about "Vengeance..." They ducked behind the porch railing, which had bushes growing in front of it that hid them until Cooper was on the steps.

Then Agent Angelwing made her move. She jumped up like a sprinter, took a running leap and launched herself at him, horizontally airborne, feet-first, and smacked a kick into the man's grizzled jaw – something cracked. He sprawled across the shallow stairs, senseless. Angelwing landed and stood tensed over him until she was sure he was out cold.

Dang! She's dangerous! Penny stared at the woman, glad she was on the same side as her. Angel grinned. "Someone had to take him out, kiddos." She looked down. "But I won't lie, that was satisfying. This creep has done a lot of wrong to people I love."

"Yeah, but wow." Blake shook his head side to side, a stunned expression glued on his face.

And then a shout. They looked up to see Markdown and Bryce, full-out running towards the house.

 "Nicely done, honey!" Markdown called out, pointing to Cooper's inert form.

Angelwing laughed. "Thanks!"

Markdown scaled the steps and swept her into a hug. Bryce came puffing up, his poor thin face sheened with sweat from the effort of running. "The missile!" He managed to speak between gasps.

Cooper's tablet had gone sliding across the porch boards and now Angelwing picked it up, and Penny looked over her shoulder to see. "LAUNCH ABORTED" popped up on the map screen.

Angel showed it to Bryce. "Your dad must have done something brilliant." He looked like he didn't know what to say, opening and closing his mouth.

Two gunshots sounded inside. Angelwing's radio buzzed. She whipped it out and answered it. "Monty! We've captured Cooper and his tablet says 'launch aborted'. What's going on?"

"A standoff. There are a few of Cooper's men in here still defending the parlor, of all places." Mr. Montrose's dry tone spilled through the speaker. "Perhaps you could persuade them to cease fire? Greg has disarmed the missile. We did it!"

An electrified whoop of victory went up around the porch. "Let's get in there!" Bryce shouted, chopping a hand towards the house and running to the front door.

Markdown slapped Cooper's cheeks until the man woke up, then dragged him, still groggy, into the house at gunpoint.

When Cooper's men realized he was in the agents' custody, the few that remained surrendered. The agents locked them in a cow shed until backup had arrived in the form of more of their International Counterintelligence & Espionage agents as well as a unit of camo-clad, helmeted, goggled SOCOM – Special Operations Command soldiers of Australia. Dust whirled around the compound from the arrival of all their vehicles. In the sky, trailing wisps of clouds were all that was left of the hurricane, and through them the stars and moon gleamed.

Objective achieved.

CHAPTER TWELVE

In the Aftermath

Cara had never been happier to see her husband, not even walking down the aisle. Running down the hallway of the ranch house to his side as he came from the parlor was a million times more exhilarating. Because he was *alive*.

"You're okay - You're *okay*! Oh thank God." She buried her face in his chest, crying because finally it was all right to let go. She didn't have to be brave anymore.

"Hey, shh." Bryce rubbed her back and kissed the top of her head. "I'm all right. I'm just glad to see you're in one piece." He fingered the bullet scratch on her vest. "Your first close call – I hope it's the last."

"Don't count on that one, son." Bryce's father spoke up from behind him. Bryce tensed and turned to look. Agents milled around them but it felt like the three of them were on their own little island of drama.

"What do you mean?"

"This lovely girl is one of the bravest women I've ever met. She would be incredible as a special Agent – the courage I saw in her today under fire was truly inspiring." Greg's face shone with – pride? "You chose the right person for your other half."

Wow. I'm so glad he approves of me!

"Well – Dad – I definitely agree with all of that." Bryce hugged her close and kissed her cheek. "Couldn't be prouder of my wife."

I think I'm gonna melt. And that had been the first time Bryce called his father "Dad" in her hearing.

"I will definitely be putting in a recommendation for her to be promoted into active agency status."

Umm – hang on a minute – just because I can doesn't mean I should! Before she could voice her concern, Bryce intervened for her. "We'll have to talk about it. But thanks, I'm sure a recommendation from you would go a long way." His expression held admiration, and he loosened his hold on her and stepped closer to his father. "Are you really the Gingerbread Man?"

Greg Reynolds nodded. "It's true."

A slow grin spread out on Bryce's face, and then he was laughing. Greg smiled back and the two men met in an embrace, just as Blake came around the corner behind them. Tears sprang into his eyes and he leaned against the wall, a fist pressed to his mouth.

And then, following him, came her best girlfriend, with a perky spring in her step that made her auburn tresses sway.

"PENNY!" Cara dashed around Bryce and Greg and caught her friend in a hug, whirling around and nearly falling. "You're okay!"

"Me? Pshaw! I was just snatched by a thug and tied up for a few hours – you were the one dumped on a deserted island for days!" Penny pulled away and looked off into the middle distance. "Come to think of it though, you did have your admittedly hot husband along. So I guess it's about even!" She squeezed Cara in one of her exuberant hugs. "I'm so glad to see you're alive! You look like you could stand a few good meals, though!"

Both of us have been through serious trials since my wedding day. But by the grace of God, here we stand, none the worse thanks to his protection. "Yeah, I could eat a horse – can't taste any worse than the crocodile meat."

Penny's jaw dropped. "You'll have to tell me that story! And also the one about how you're actually married to a secret agent and *didn't tell me!*" She turned white and gasped. "Wait, you knew he was, right?"

Cara laughed loud and long. *Oh Penny. You have no idea.* "Yes! Of course I did!"

Then Penny smacked her jokingly on the arm. "And why didn't you let me know Blake was moving to Peachtree City?!"

She gasped. "I didn't tell you?! Oh, I thought I had! Must have been bridal-brain." Cara let some giggles escape like bubbles floating in the air. "But hey, he's not so bad, huh?"

"Shhh!" Penny looked in Blake's direction, but he was now talking with his father and Bryce. "I know, right?" She opened her eyes wide and cocked an eyebrow. "We'll talk." She nodded several times and then headed over to the trio of Reynolds men and slipped her hand into Blake's.

Whoo! That's promising! Cara eyed her friend, who looked at her and blushed, a pretty smile making her freckles dance.

They were just in time to see Bryce turn to Blake and smile, his face open and eyes full of gratitude. "Hey man – thanks for what you did back there on the boat. If you hadn't mediated between me and Dad – we could never have pulled this off together."

Blake leaned back against the hallway wall, putting a hand to his forehead. "So that's it!"

They stared at him until he shook his head and explained. "I didn't know why I had to come, but for some reason, I did, I could feel it – and that was why... to bring you and Dad back together." The realization dawned on his face, bright and shining.

Bryce nodded. "Yeah, and if it had been anyone but you, I might not have listened."

Cara smiled against her husband's shoulder. She understood. *Blake has been there through it all with him – the years their father was gone.*

And then Mr. Montrose appeared, at last wearing a pleased expression behind his square-lensed glasses. He cleared his throat and clasped his hands behind his back. "A few announcements." He started, looking around at the circle. Out of nowhere, Angelwing and Markdown materialized and hovered at his elbows.

"I am pleased to announce that *all* of you – Ashburn, Diamond, Gingerbread Man, Angelwing, Markdown, and even you, Blake, are receiving special commendations for 'Extreme Bravery' from the ICE Agency international headquarters." He clapped his chocolate-tinted hands. "Well done, all of you." Then he looked at Penny. "And may I say, Miss Marshall, that I am very glad to see you are none the worse for your abduction ordeal."

"Thank you, sir." Penny nodded. "Wait, who are Ashburn and Diamond? I've heard the other names, but..."

She and Bryce shared a look. His eyes danced in amusement, then he raised his hand. "The first would be me, Penny, that's my code name. As for Diamond – that's the handle Monty assigned to Cara here after our adventures in Europe, although she doesn't have official 'agent' status."

Penny's jaw dropped. "Wow!"

Then Mr. Montrose actually laughed. "Oh, and Bryce and Cara – the Turtle Bay Resort in Oahu felt so badly about what happened to you that they're offering to completely refund your honeymoon *and* give you another week's stay for free."

Cara gasped and looked up at Bryce. *How generous of them!*

He grinned. "What a nice gesture."

She tugged at his jumpsuit and pulled him away from the others. "Let's talk about that for a second."

He nodded. "All right." He looked back to say "Hey, guys, everyone went above and beyond today. You're the best." A chorus of thanks went up, with return remarks that so had he.

Bryce walked with her outside and they strolled along, arms loosely entwined. The sun had set and the sky was unleashing a dazzling array of starlight. "What is it, my Diamond?" He playfully used her code name.

"Well, that was very sweet of the resort to offer that extra week, but I want to take a rain check."

He stopped walking, surprise immobilizing him. "Really? I thought you'd jump at the chance for more luxury and pampering." He winked.

She smiled and tugged him closer, lifting her chin for a kiss. He obliged.

"My love, I just want to go home." She traced her fingertips along his square jawline, smooth once more. He'd shaved off the rough stubble on the Agency boat on the way to the ranch. "...and home is wherever you are."

He let out a sigh of relief and closed his eyes. "I love that we're on the same page." He opened his eyes, a flame of inspiration glowing in them. "Let's go back to your – make that *our*, apartment in Atlanta." He traced the curve of her cheek with his nose, then whispered in her ear. "We'll watch old movies, lie on the couch together and just hide from the outside world for a while."

That... sounds SO perfect.

"Have I told you lately how much I absolutely adore you?"

After Cara left with Bryce, Penny realized a talk with Blake was definitely in order as well. "Feel like exploring the stables?" She invited, hearing a note of softness in her own voice.

"Yeah – that sounds good." Blake smiled gently at her – not his usual melon-slice grin, but a small, curious half-smile. "Shoulda figured we couldn't keep you away from the animals long."

"If you see a dog roaming around, let me know." Greg looked concerned. "I'm not sure where my sheepdog went, but if he's okay he'll turn up."

They promised to do so. As they walked out of the house, they passed by Angelwing, who winked at Penny behind Blake's back and formed the shape of a heart with her fingers. Penny rolled her eyes at her and smiled.

They entered the night outside, listening to the hum of insects. The air was cooling a bit from the dry heat. Penny started humming, then choked when she realized the song in her head was "Can you feel the love tonight?" Thankfully, she'd only made it past the first three notes. *I hope Blake didn't recognize it!*

"You ok?" Blake looked concerned, which made her giggle, which she had to cough to cover up.

"Yes!" She squeaked after finally gasping in some air. "Just fine. Sorry!"

He laughed. "No problem."

They reached the stable and for a few minutes she was distracted, loving on the horses and patting their noses. They were down-to-earth boys and girls, just typical quarter horses used to working hard, but she thought they were sweet.

While they were in the stable, an Australian sheepdog appeared. It had been hiding in one of the stalls. He frolicked around them, panting happily and lolling his tongue. Blake looked relieved. "We'll have to let my dad know this guy is all right."

Eventually, she and Blake wandered out to a grove of citrus trees and stopped, standing in the moonlight that cast violet shadows around them.

He gazed down at her, eyes holding deep wells of tenderness. She held her breath as he leaned closer and pressed his lips against her forehead in a sweet, soft kiss.

She hoped he couldn't hear her heart pounding like a herd of galloping horses.

When he lifted his head, she found her voice. "I have something to tell you."

His expression was open and ready. "Mmmhmm?"

"I…" *Oh lord. Help me find the words to express what's in my heart.* She took a steadying breath. "I think – " He waited, patient and sweet, until she could get the words out.

"– I think my heart is ready for a new adventure."

Joy instantly radiated across his face, as if an extra portion of moonlight had spilled onto this very spot where they stood.

"Penny." He clasped both of her hands in his and held them up to his chest between them. "I would do… *anything*… to be part of that adventure." Earnest promise vibrated in his tone.

A sob got stuck on its way out of her throat, and she rested her cheek against Blake's solid chest. *Safe. Secure.*

She sniffed back the tears threatening to fall. *I'll always remember you, Mason. But I can't live in the past. And I'm thinking that you wouldn't want me to.* A bright new beginning glowed ahead of her.

He tipped up her chin with one finger. "Tears?"

She smiled and blinked away the droplets. "Happy ones."

"Ahh." He curled his arms around her shoulders and held her gently. "The best kind." He rocked back and forth, and she felt as comforted as if she were in a cradle. "You know, to even be talking about adventures after the day we've had is evidence of just how special and spunky you are."

She blushed. "Well – I'm not the one who got a special commendation for bravery, mister. That was you all the way, you and the secret agents. And Cara, who's like half-a-secret-agent-"

He laughed. "By all rights, you should have one too. Seriously, Penny. Your spirit is so colorful and courageous. It inspires me."

She inhaled a long breath. "Blake! That's the most amazing thing to say."

"But it's so true." He grinned, excitement evidenced in his dimples. "I can't wait to discover even more about you."

"You've got surprises too, buster. Like several special agents in your family!"

"-Hey, even I didn't know about those!"

Greg looked around the less-crowded hall. His sons and their ladies had left him, Monty, and the two agents Angelwing and Markdown standing there.

Markdown turned to him, a question on his fine-boned face. "Sir, is it true you and your team once hacked into an Al Qaeda website and replaced sixty-seven pages of bomb-making instructions with a cupcake recipe?"

Angelwing smacked her husband on the arm. "Mark!" She reprimanded, looking embarrassed, "That's one of the silliest rumors floating around the Agency!"

"No, it's not true." Greg shook his head.

Angel eyed Markdown, her face saying *See?* Markdown looked crestfallen until Greg spoke again. "It wasn't *my team* – just me."

Angelwing's eyes popped wide and she clapped a hand over her mouth, while Markdown laughed, gently elbowing his wife in the side. "See, honey? I knew it was real."

Monty coughed. "Anything you hear about the Gingerbread man, add several outlandish details and then it'll be close to the truth." He shooed the two younger agents away with his hands. "Scurry off now, Ginger and I need to talk."

They brought themselves up short and stood straighter, laughter dissolving. "Yes sir!" They moved off and joined the swirl of wrap-up activity.

"What do we need to talk about?" Greg asked, "-or would it be better to adjourn to my room?"

Monty's dark eyes were solemn. "Let's." He nodded for Greg to lead the way, and they removed themselves from the hubbub. Greg closed the door behind them. He looked up at his longtime friend, who stood with his hands clasped behind his back.

"It's time for you to come home." Monty's gravelly voice was dead serious.

"No! I can't. It's not safe." *The man who blackmailed me into leaving the agency is still out there.*

"That's what you think." Monty's face cleared of its frown. "Just listen. Months ago, your son Bryce led the raid on a fortress where we encountered those behind the black-market arms dealers operating under the front of Ravenmeister, Inc. – Ryan Black and his partner, Tatiana Kovalchick."

Greg shook his head. "I know. Black apparently leapt to his death on the rocks of the Mosel river. But the body was never recovered."

"He never resurfaced. On the river, or in the black market. We've had our eyes and ears out double-time ever since his fall, and none of his previous activity has been resumed." Monty's smile spread wide. "You can relax, Greg. The man's gone for good. Trust me, if he was alive and up to his old tricks, we'd know it. He poses no threat to you anymore."

Greg ruffled his hands through his hair and paced around the room, turned to stare at Montrose. "Is it safe for my family, if I return?"

Montrose sighed, closing his eyes, then opening them. "You know life never offers a 100% guarantee. But the chances are good – better than they've been in the past ten years. It's time."

It's time. The beautiful thought echoed in his brain like bells ringing in a cathedral.

He was going home.

Greg watched the clouds swoosh past from his view in the private jet high above them. The plane cruised through the sky like a silent shark, holding 18 passengers in its leather-skinned belly. It felt like he had been away from home for a thousand years instead of ten. And they still had 15 hours left of their 19-plus hour trip from Sydney to Atlanta, with one stopover in Honolulu.

He and his sons would have lots of time to make up for lost time – and he was eager to hear about everything that had happened in their lives while he was gone. But right now they slept in their seats, each next to the women they loved. Bryce pillowed Cara's head on his shoulder, while Blake held Penny's hand in his as they dreamed.

Markdown and Angelwing weren't asleep quite yet, they were still at work, laptops in front of them as they wrote up mission reports, but from the yawns and the way Markdown was rubbing his eyes, it looked like they were headed that way soon. He admired the bravery and diligence the pair exhibited. They, the next crop of agents, would hold the world together – a relief, since his generation was gone or retired.

Three happy couples in front of his eyes. Seemed he and Montrose were the odd ducks, and even Monty had a faithful wife, Jennifer, waiting for him back in D.C.

Dawn. His forever-darling. He still remembered, with vivid clarity, the night she'd told him, dewy-eyed, they were going to be parents – and nine short months later, welcomed a baby son they'd named Bryce Gregory Reynolds.

But loneliness had been a part of him for so long that it felt as if it was permanently attached to his heart. If removed, could he survive it? Was he truly a "lone wolf"? But warring against it was the longing – that aching desire for love and warmth and companionship. The things he'd shared with his wife.

What was the state of her heart? Did she wait for him with open arms, as Blake had, or was she enclosed in walls of bitterness and hurt as Bryce was before the raid on the ranch?

He wouldn't blame her, if that were the case. Not at all.

Suddenly the hours until they would arrive in Atlanta seemed all too short, if they were all that separated him from cold rejection.

They passed quickly though, after he slept for a good eight hours and then spent the next morning and noon laughing and talking with his sons, who freely shared the memories he hadn't been there to experience.

He followed the others down the ramp and into the Atlanta airport, which teemed with life like a pond crowded with tadpoles – everyone moving and flowing in a current of purpose.

The sounds weren't quite reaching his ears, as if he was encased in a solitary bubble the sound waves didn't penetrate. He searched for the familiar face that had floated in and out of his dreams for a decade.

Then – there. She hurried towards them through the crowds with her gliding steps that always made him think she was ice-skating rather than walking. And at his wife's side – a slim, beautiful young lady with dark hair, heart-shaped face, and his own pale-blue eyes. *Bethany! Oh my. She's a young woman now.*

"Gregory!" Dawn cried out, her eyes pooling with tears, running to him – with open arms.

His heart was going to burst, he knew it, for how would it hold all this joy and gratefulness, and *love?*

He swept her into his embrace and held her tight, but gently, for fear this beautiful creature would disappear like a mirage. But no, she remained, and kissed him with a passion that took his breath away.

When they pulled back to look at each other face-to-face, he took a deep breath – and realized he could breathe freely for the first time in a *long* time.

"Greg! I can't believe you're here!" She held his face in her hands, eyes shining.

He couldn't talk. No. Or his throat would emit the croaks of the ancient bullfrog and he would die of shame. But talk he must. "Dawn!" He could talk! And it didn't even sound horrible. "Sweetheart – I love you so much. I've missed you *so much!*"

But another woman waited for his attention – Bethany, lingering behind her mother with wide eyes and a wondering expression, with no smile to be seen. With a pang that hurt all the way to his core, he realized his daughter didn't know him. He'd aged since she was a little girl of eight, but surely not that much...

"Dad?" Her lower lip quivered.

"It's me." He let go of Dawn with one hand and extended it to Bethany. "You've grown – into a beautiful young lady." She moved forward and lifted her arms around him, accepting his hug, but it was cool, lacking the fervent warmth of Dawn's welcome.

That was all right. Bethany would obviously take a little longer to warm to him, but he was more than willing to be patient and win back his daughter's affection.

The rest of their traveling group had watched the scene play out with varying degrees of emotion and empathy. He looked at his two strapping sons. "Come here, boys! Family hug!"

The five of them crowded together in one solid connection. The entire Reynolds family, reunited at long last. Over Blake's shoulder, he could see Cara crying and clinging to Penny, who had her phone out and was snapping pictures as fast as she could.

Bless her! If any moment in history was picture-worthy, this was. *Surely, God's in his heaven and all's right with the world. Otherwise, how could this have worked out so perfectly?*

244

Greg felt as if he had been welcomed back into the fold – lone wolf no more, but lost lamb who had been restored to love and safety.

After they had all gathered themselves together and wiped their wet faces, Monty shook his hand, a smile spreading under his close-cropped moustache. "Take care, Greg. We'll be in touch." He and the other agents left to catch another flight to D.C. and return to the Agency underground headquarters below the publishing house front.

Bryce had eaten three chicken sandwiches and was on his fourth, squeezed into a corner booth next to his wife and his family in the Chick-fil-A Dwarf House close to the Atlanta airport. They'd all quickly decided on the restaurant and now laughed and ate together before he and Cara left for their apartment and the others for Peachtree City. Blake surprised them with the announcement that he'd bought a rental property – a beautiful three-bedroom home with a pool, perfect for his parents and Bethany to stay in for as long as they wished. His mother insisted they pay a fair rent but was more than pleased with the arrangement.

Cara took a long sip of her frozen lemonade and closed her eyes in bliss. "Heaven." She declared, sipping again. "I'd like to hug whoever invented this!"

"I heard it was a group of teenage employees!" Penny giggled. "The little geniuses."

As Blake started telling the story of how he used to combine every different soda from the soft-drink fountain, Bryce flicked his gaze around the restaurant. Agent Shadowchaser sat a mere fifteen feet away at another table, nursing a sweet tea, and two other agents blended into the surroundings. They'd been at the airport too, and had tailed them here. A security blanket for his family.

Bryce pulled out his new phone that Monty had bestowed on him as a replacement for the one he'd lost and texted Trent's number.

[BRYCE REYNOLDS]: You've been keeping an eye on Mom & B?

Trent pulled out his phone, read the screen, tapped a message back.

[TRENT THATCHER]: Yeah. They've been safe while U were gone.

[BRYCE REYNOLDS]: Thanks man. I O U one.

Trent grinned.

[TRENT THATCHER]: No way. Score isn't even settled yet, not after Moscow. U don't owe me anything.

[BRYCE REYNOLDS]: Just doing my job.

[TRENT THATCHER]: Same here. Glad you're alive, btw.

[BRYCE REYNOLDS]: LOL - Me too!

Cara elbowed him, peeking over his shoulder. "Who are you texting?"

"It's work-related." He said that for the benefit of the others at the table, but leaned close to her ear and whispered "Agent Shadowchaser at ten o'clock."

Trent winked at Cara as her gaze found him and nodded.

She smiled. Then she turned to Penny before the others realized what had transpired. "So, you two." She waved a finger back and forth between Penny and Blake, who sat with Blake's arm around Penny's shoulders. "When did this happen?"

Penny blushed, but a smile teased at her mouth. Blake puffed his chest out and grinned openly. "Well – you both went off and got married, and left us behind all lonely and such – so really it's your fault."

"I take full credit!" Cara smirked. "Even though I had nothing to do with it!"

Laughter tumbled around the table.

They pulled up to the house in Blake's SUV, and Greg couldn't hold back the sigh of happiness. It was a sweet home with a pool in the backyard and roses and honeysuckle growing on the mailbox – which Dawn was already gushing over. "It's gorgeous, honey!" She hugged Blake around the neck.

"Well, it needs a few updates but it'll be a great rental investment. And in the meantime, while you're all getting your bearings, it'll be a good spot for ya'll to just rest for a while."

Rest? I hardly remember the word.

Now that they were in Georgia once more, Blake slipped back to his "southern-realtor" voice as he gave them a tour.

After hugs all around, Blake left to take Penny home and then crash at his own apartment, leaving them to spend the rest of the evening alone – him, his wife, and their daughter.

Bethany had laughed and joked with her brothers, but avoided his gaze the whole late-afternoon and evening. She didn't speak to her mother, either. Now that they'd seen the whole house, Bethany retreated upstairs to her bedroom and closed the door with a gentle 'click'.

His wife smiled sadly. "Give her time." She shook her head. "This has been a big mental adjustment for her."

"I'll wait for her as long as she needs me to." He took his wife's hand in his and tugged her towards the back door. "Just like you waited for me."

They shared a loving glance, and gratitude poured over him again. "Come – walk with me." He invited. They stepped out into the backyard patio, and the scent of the freshly-cut grass drifted to them on the breeze.

"I know you must wonder why I left – and what I was doing."

"Yes." She frankly admitted, but ran her hand over his shoulder in a caress and added "But I *know* you. So I know you must have had a darn good reason. All these years, that knowledge is what kept me going."

Her faith in him was awe-inspiring. The only thing Dawn had known about his work that it was for the government and it was classified.

He stopped walking at the edge of the pool and drew her close, resting his forehead against hers. "I'll probably never be able to reveal the details, but I was targeted by a group of enemy counterintelligence agents in a retaliatory strike. For the safety of you and the children, I had to distance myself from you and go dark-"

"Oh my!" His wife's eyes were wide, looking up at him in amazement.

"-But I used it for a good purpose. While I was undercover and cut off from everyone at the Agency besides Montrose, I managed to complete five hugely important missions. Working for Cooper was the sixth."

"Bravo, sweetheart." Dawn slipped her arms around him. "What's next for you? Will you be retiring?" Hope glimmered in her face.

He'd been thinking about that all the way home. *It's time. Time I slowed down and finally rested.* The younger generation of smart, capable agents had arisen, ready to take the mantle of responsibility from him and his counterparts.

"Yes." He nodded, feeling laughter welling up inside. He let it out. *"Yes!* I'm retiring."

Mischief danced in her hazel eyes. "Well then, mister. It's time you got started having fun." She slipped her hand into the pocket of his khakis and grabbed his cell phone, then suddenly she shoved him off-balance and he fell into the pool, fully dressed! "Ker-splash"!

The cool water embraced him, bubbles tickling his face and arms, and he resurfaced to hear his wife cackling with laughter. Her face was creased, eyes closed, arms closed over her ribs like her sides were splitting.

"You little-" He rushed to the pool's edge and bounded out like a sea monster, sloshing water all over the patio. Dawn squealed and tried to run for it, but all he let her do was toss their cell phones safely on the padded outdoor couch before he grabbed her around the waist and carried her, kicking and shrieking, to the pool and plopped her in.

Their laughter and splashing brought Bethany to her upstairs window. "Mom? Dad?!" She looked shocked and embarrassed, staring at her parents cavorting in the water. "What are you doing?!"

"Get used to it, honey!" her mother called. "Things are going to be a lot more fun from here on out. Why don't you join us?!"

Bethany shook her head, but a hint of a smile touched her lips. "Maybe later." She closed her curtains.

"Progress! I like it." He winked at his drenched wife.

Everything's going to be just fine. Thank you, God.

"Honey?" Bryce's voice echoed from the kitchen of their cozy, well-decorated apartment. "Do you want ice cream or steak for lunch – or perhaps both?!" His rich laugh followed the words.

She rolled over on the couch and paused the episode of *Agatha Christie's Poirot.* "Ugh, maybe just a salad? We've been eating so much food for the past few days!" *And relaxing. And spending time alone. And watching WAY too much Netflix.*

"I know! Isn't it awesome?" A short while later, he came out with two trays – one with a chicken Caesar salad on it for her, and one with steak, ice cream, and a bowl of chili on it for himself.

"Thanks sweetie. You're the best." She dug into her fresh, crunchy salad and pressed play. Poirot had everyone assembled and was about to reveal who the murderer was.

But before he could, their phone trilled. Bryce groaned and answered it. She paused the TV.

"Hello?" Bryce listened for a moment. "Both of us? All right, let me put you on speaker."

He hit the button and Mr. Montrose's dry voice continued speaking. "Yes. Cara, are you there?"

"Yes sir!" *Please don't say Bryce has to come back to work yet...*

"Good. I need to talk to you two." He sounded like he was shuffling papers. "If you recall, Cara has a standing offer from the Agency for a part-time position, but it's just been upgraded to full-time with benefits after a sparkling recommendation came in from one Greg Reynolds, whose word carries a whole lot of weight with the international board."

Cara's heart raced. *A full-time special agent? It's exciting, but – I'm not ready!* "But sir..."

"I'm not quite finished." Mr. Montrose took a sip of something – probably black coffee. He'd be on his third or fourth mug by now. "This position would only be available after Cara goes through extensive physical training, and a crash course at the Academy. But she would be assigned as your permanent partner, Bryce."

Oh. I... I could DO that. In fact, the thought exhilarated her.

"Wow." Bryce finally spoke. His face was drawn and tight. "We'll have to call you back, Monty." He hung up.

"My goodness." Cara set aside her bowl of salad. "This is amazing!"

He looked at her, ashen. "This is horrible."

"What? Why?!" *Don't you want me working with you?*

"I would die if you got killed in action as a secret agent." He got off the couch and knelt in front of her, clasping her hands.

"Likewise." She murmured softly. "And I know you're not going to stop anytime soon."

That made him look off to the side, then he fastened his gaze on her again. "I know. But the risks are so huge —"

"Bryce... I know this is scary for you to wrap your mind around. But I want to do this." She let her determination bleed through into her tone. "I want to be by your side. Defeat the badguys together. I want to watch your back, just like on the last mission." She stroked his hands with hers, then pulled them to her lips. "You could train me – teach me everything you know."

"That's a lot. Just saying." He shrugged.

"I know. But our life looks like it's going to be dangerous, anyway – I mean, look what happened on our honeymoon! And we weren't even on a mission!"

He sighed and closed his eyes, bowed his head.

She waited a few minutes. "Are you praying or thinking?"

"Both." He lifted his head, eyes open. "What about our future children?"

Her stomach flip-flopped in nervousness. "I know. We promised each other not to be on active duty as parents." She took a deep breath. "We'll have to wait and see how long it takes. Once the kids come, so do the desk jobs. I'll go back to graphic design from home and you can become a consultant for the Agency."

His eyebrows lifted in interest. "I hadn't thought of applying for that. Sure would beat paperwork."

She smiled. "So... are we agreed?"

"We are." He leaned closer. "But I think we should seal it with a kiss." So they did.

She came up for air a moment later. "But shouldn't we call Monty back right away?"

He kissed her nose. "Later."

She giggled. "Your ice cream is melting."

That stopped him, but only for a second. "I'll drink it with a straw."

Epilogue

THREE MONTHS LATER

Penny couldn't decide. The white lace dress was brand-new, but she wasn't sure what jewelry and shoes to pair with the vintage-style garment. The old favorite floral was a little worn, but she already knew it looked good on her and what shoes and jewelry to accessorize.

This calls for bestie input. She snatched her phone from the side-table next to her bed and dialed Cara.

"Hello?" Cara's sweet voice answered.

"New Lace dress, or old floral fave?" She picked up Dot right before the little claws could snag the fabric of the lace dress, and put the kitty in her basket. She snuggled down for a nap.

"Definitely the new lace one! And wear that coral necklace I gave you!" Cara always knew what jewelry to wear. It was one of her fashion strengths.

"I hadn't thought of that. Shoes?" Penny grabbed the necklace from her jewelry box.

"Hmm..." Cara sounded like she was cooking in her kitchen. "Hang on a second, I have to get these potatoes in the oven to roast." A few moments later after the bang of the oven door was heard, her friend was back on the line. "Do you still have those flats with the gems on the toes?"

"Yes, but they're all different colors – oh wait, there's coral in them." Penny laid the shoes and the necklace on her bed next to the dress. "Perfect! I love you!"

"My pleasure! What's the occasion?"

"Blake has invited me to dinner. Apparently he's grilling salmon."

"Oooh! I'd *fish* for an invitation, pardon the pun, hah-hah-"

"Oh that one was baaaad. Ugh."

Cara giggled. "-but I have a roast in the crockpot and Bryce has been looking forward to it all day. Besides, you and Blake need some space."

Blake. Three months into dating him, and still the thought of him gave her butterflies. "Cara... he's so wonderful."

"I know it, darling, I married his older brother, who is very much like him!"

"That you did." Penny hung the floral dress back in the closet and held the lace one up to her, spinning in front of the mirror.

"Well I hope you have a wonderful evening with your wonderful date – my wonderful hubby just got home, so I'll let you go."

"Okay then. Thanks again for the invaluable advice!" Penny had been about to ask for makeup and hairstyle suggestions, but she could always hit her Pinterest board for inspiration.

They said their goodbyes and Penny tucked her phone in her gigantic peach leather purse, which went wherever she did. It allowed her to carry a pad of paper and pencils in case she ever needed to sketch out an idea for a painting that wouldn't wait.

After consulting Pinterest, she tamed her curls with a half-updo, leaving her auburn hair free to cascade down her back, and went with just a touch of soft copper eye shadow, donned the rest of the outfit, and decided to take her car over to Blake's apartment instead of the golf cart. *No road dust shall mar the utter creamy perfection of this lace dress!*

The evening light was coming in through the window *just right* on the table he'd set for dinner. The salmon would be perfect in just a few minutes, already drizzled with lemon juice and seasoned with an array of secret spices.

And the most important thing, the hidden camera in the potted tree, was ready to go.

Then the doorbell rang. His nerves tingled and he straightened his bowtie. Ran a hand through his hair. He swung open the door and there she stood in all her glory, dark-red hair gleaming in the setting sun. She was all prettied-up... had done something special to her eyes, and wore a creamy white dress that looked fantastic.

"Hey Blake!" She walked in, smiling up at him. Up close, her tiny freckles looked like angel-glitter sprinkled all over her cheeks. In her hand, she carried a loaf of her crusty homemade bread he loved. "I thought this could go with dinner."

She's breathtaking.

His throat was dry. He grinned, hoping she wouldn't notice he was mute as a fish – *Oh! The salmon filets!* "Make yourself at home, I'll get the food off the grill." He dashed out the back door.

He took a moment to compose himself as he carefully arranged the grilled fish on a platter. He was taking his third deep breath when he heard her voice behind him. "Can I do anything to help?"

Blake nearly dropped the platter, but instead caught it in an ungraceful staggering motion. "Uh – uh yeah, you can get the salad out of the fridge."

She giggled. "You sure are jumpy tonight." With a swish of her skirt, she disappeared from the doorframe.

He'd better get it together or she would guess what he had planned.

Blake carried the salmon into the dining room and laid it on the table between their plates. He just managed to turn on the camera before Penny brought the salad in from the kitchen. "It looks delicious, babe." She smiled appreciatively. "Gotta love a man who can cook!"

He laughed and waved it off as if it was no big deal. *Really? Do you love me? I hope so.*

Because I love you.

They seated themselves and he prayed over the food, no shorter nor longer than he usually did. *Can't tip her off yet.*

Penny took one bite of the salmon he'd grilled and squeaked with her mouth closed, flapping her hand. "Mmmm!!"

"Oh gosh, what's wrong with it?" *I've ruined everything-!*

She stared at him, swallowed, laughed. "Nothing! It's *so* good! What in the world did you put on it?"

He sighed in relief, hoping his face wasn't red from his racing heartbeat. "Secret spices."

She grinned. "Oh, I see how it is." She leaned towards him. "You're going to make me beg for the recipe." She pouted her lips. "Pleeeease?"

He laughed – she was so full of fun! Her antics always made him smile. "Oh, okay. I'll give it to you."

Here It is. The moment. "Actually – I have something else for you too." His dining table had two drawers on each end for silverware, and that's where he'd hidden it.

He opened the drawer and pulled out the huge single deep red rose. *To symbolize true love.*

She took the flower from him in awe, bringing it to her nose to smell the deep, sweet fragrance – which was when she noticed the sparkle of the ring tucked in the very center of the petals.

One cushion-cut morganite stone glittered a soft peachy-pink, set in a curvy scalloped setting of rose-gold edged in tiny diamonds. He'd thought it the embodiment of everything Penny was – warm and sweet and unique.

Her sharp intake of air made his insides quiver. "Ohhhh!"

He laid his napkin on the table and stood, kneeling in front of her on one knee and reaching for her hands. He took the ring from her and held it by the delicate band.

"I know we've only been dating for three months, but I don't want to wait for our forever." He took one more deep breath. "Penelope Elizabeth Marshall, I love you with everything inside me."

Her lips trembled and she hid them with her free hand, eyes wide with tears welling up in them. But she responded. "Blake – I love you too." She smiled as she told him.

His heart gave a huge leap, like a balloon cut free from its tether, soaring up into the blue sky. "I was hoping you'd say that." They both laughed. Then he continued.

"You are the sweetest, spunkiest woman I've ever seen on God's green earth, so full of fun and color. You light up my world. I'm attracted to you on so many levels, that I can't help but think God has perfectly crafted us for each other. I think He brought us together, and I believe he's got a wonderful future planned for us, better than we can even imagine."

She nodded, tears slipping off her cheeks like crystal raindrops.

"So, Penny...will you marry me?"

"YES!" She hopped to her feet. "Oh gosh yes! Yes-yes-yes!"

He leapt to his feet and she slipped her arms around his neck and they embraced each other, standing there while the last golden sunlight poured through the windows. "I love you so much!" She sobbed against him.

He rubbed her back in slow circles. "Shhh, it's okay. I love you too!"

She tilted her tear-streaked face up to him. "I. Am. So. Blessed." She sniffed. "I've loved and lost Mason, and I never thought I'd find another man like him – but I didn't have to! God had you find me. And everything's different, but so beautiful.""

"Just so you know, my love, I'm not taking his place in your heart – just making my own place." He stroked his thumb over her cheek, erasing a tear-trail. "I won't be hurt by your memories of him. I wish I could have known him too. And we'll see him someday again on those streets of gold. Until then, I have the precious job of taking care of you."

That started Penny crying again. "You are such a good man!"

"And you are an amazing woman that I'm thrilled will be my wife – very soon, I hope." He held up the ring again. "Let's see if it fits!"

"Oh!" Penny gasped again as he slid the circlet of rose-gold onto her slim, short finger. It looked at home on her small hand and fit perfectly. "Blake, it's absolutely gorgeous."

261

"I saw it on Etsy and knew it was yours." He'd picked it out himself. But before buying, he'd checked with his brother, who had given him a thumbs-up. He trusted Bryce's judgment because the ring he'd chosen for Cara had been beyond perfect for her.

"Um – I love you." She nodded. "Like, a *lot*."

"Same back – so let's get married!"

"Ohmygoodness. We're getting married. We're getting MARRIED!" She squealed and hugged him again. "I'm so happy!"

"So am I!" *Incredibly, overpoweringly happy! She loves me!*

"Oh, and I'm so glad you didn't do the whole treasure-hunt thing that Bryce did when he proposed. Cara loved it, but this way – personal and private – is exactly what I wanted." Penny thanked him, gratefulness emanating from her. "But do you think we should take a selfie or something?"

"I did one better." He looked at the potted tree. "Smile for the camera!" He grinned and waved at the lens, barely visible through the leaves.

Penny gushed out a flood of laughter, pointing at the tree. "That was so smart!" She smiled and waved.

"We'll be able to take frames from the footage and print them out, as well as watch the tape." Blake walked over and turned off the camera.

Penny looked at the table. "Oh dear – we'd better finish our food, it's probably getting cold!"

"Care to talk wedding plans over the rest of dinner?"

"I know." Penny clasped her hands. "Let's elope!"

"Can't, my mom would kill me!" They laughed together. "We could get married next week though."

"Seriously? You would do that – for me?"

"In a heartbeat."

Cara stretched her sore muscles as she limped into Bryce's Agency D.C. apartment. It had been a long morning of kicking and punching at the Agency gym, but they'd gone home for lunch and showers. Bryce could be a really tough taskmaster, pushing her to be her best – and then a little bit more. But having his insight was priceless. He only asked the harder hits from her because he knew someday she'd need the ability to do it. *When that day comes, I want to be ready.*

Plus, now she had killer abs.

Her phone rang, and she looked longingly towards the shower. Oddly enough, Bryce's cell rang at nearly the same moment. He walked into the bedroom to answer it. Cara looked at her phone screen. "PENNY MARSHALL" was calling. *Yep, better answer this.*

"Well hey, girlie! I forgot to call and ask how your date with Blake went last night – how was it?"

"Well – HE PROPOSED!" Penny's voice climbed to a joyful shout.

Cara yelled at the top of her lungs, falling on her living room couch. "*Aaaaaah!* Oh wow! What did you say?!" an echoing whoop sounded from the bedroom. Bryce must be talking to his brother.

"I said yes, of *course*." Penny giggled. "I'm texting you a picture of the ring."

Cara opened the photo and shrieked at the sight of the ring that could not have been *more* perfect for Penny. "It's so beautiful!"

"I know – I love it!" She cleared her throat. "Now, let's get down to business. You're my Matron of Honor, and Bryce has to be best man."

"Yes, ma'am!" She giggled. "We'd be honored."

"The thing is... the wedding is on the twenty-third."

"Okay, of what month?"

"...*This* month."

Cara gasped. "Penny! That's next Saturday!"

"I know! We almost decided to elope, but then we realized we couldn't do that to our families. It's only going to be family there, very small. I'm calling it a Weddelope." Penny laughed.

"That... is so you." Penny had such flair with words. "Well, we'd better get busy planning this if we only have... eight days and nineteen hours, if I stay up until 11:00 tonight!"

"I'm counting on you to help me pull this off – if anyone can do it, it's you!" Penny's voice rang with confidence.

"Just you wait, girlfriend. You'll have the cutest Weddelope ever."

Thank God, it's not raining. The backup plan was to get married at their church fellowship hall, if the weather failed them. But the sky was hazy, filtering the sunlight down into her little backyard and softening all the shadows.

The photographer she and Blake had chosen was ecstatic, saying the pictures would be gorgeous. *I hope so. I want some special memories of this day!*

Penny pressed her hand to her middle, trying to calm her flip-flopping stomach as she sat on the edge of her bed, dressed in all her bridal finery. Cara had worked wonders on her hair, fitting the crown of vines and rosebuds atop a beautiful up-do, filmy veil trailing down the back. Her best friend had taken the week off from her agency training to fly down to Georgia to help Penny pull together the wedding.

A tap came at her door. "It's me!" Cara's voice. Her friend cracked the door open and peeked through. "We're ready for the "first look!"

Penny followed her friend to the front door. "All the family is waiting in the backyard, leaving the side yard here private for you, Blake, and the photographer." Cara's hurried whisper explained as she guided Penny around the corner. "Go! Dazzle him!" She gave her one last gentle nudge and then vanished back into the house.

Penny gripped her bouquet and stepped towards Blake, who waited near her camellia bush with his back turned. She saw the photographer out of the corner of her eye, leaning against the fence and ready to snap pictures of her and Blake with the backdrop of the brick wall of her house behind them.

She tiptoed through the grass – mown short, for once! – and tapped her groom on his broad shoulder.

He turned, and a thousand rainbows couldn't have shone brighter than his face as he looked at her.

"Penny!" His voice came out in a whoosh, and he took a step back. "You're exquisite!"

He looks so handsome himself, in that gray suit and with his hair combed up. She could feel herself blushing. "Can you believe it? We're getting married!"

His dimples showed alongside his huge melon-slice grin. "I can't believe it. Come here." He embraced her gently, and the camera rapid-fire clicked in the background.

Don't cry. Don't cry. Do NOT ruin this marvelous makeup. She smiled instead. "I love you."

"I love you too!" He held her at arm's length, gaze sweeping her dress. "That gown is amazing!"

"I'm so glad you like it!" She stroked the chiffon tea-length skirt of the off-white dress, which she and Cara had discovered in a darling boutique. A light peach ribbon served as a sash and tied with a bow in the back, matching the tiny roses in her crown.

The photographer had them pose a few different ways together, and then left them alone for a moment to go let the violinist and the minister know they were ready to start the ceremony.

They took the opportunity to pray together for their marriage, asking the Lord to guide their steps as husband and wife. Bryce and Cara joined them at the side of the house and whispered their congratulations, hugs all around.

The elegant strains of violin music drifting from the backyard changed to "Jesu, Joy of Man's desiring"

Bryce and Cara walked out first, as Matron of Honor and Best Man.

"Ready?" Blake asked, tucking her arm around his elbow.

"Ready." She smiled as they walked around back corner of the house.

Ribbon-decked chairs lined the short expanse of lawn, with a path down the center scattered with rose petals. Underneath the spreading oak tree, a white wooden frame swathed with huge swooping lengths of beige burlap and creamy tulle served as a backdrop, in front of which the minister and Bryce and Cara waited for them.

They walked down the aisle between the guests, arm-in-arm. Penny smiled at the Reynolds side and then turned to look at – her side. The Marshalls.

The only downside to having a family-only wedding was that... they'd had to invite her family. And they came – Her divorced parents, Lyndy, Bluebell and Bluebell's husband, Ricardo the shoe salesman.

To her shock, her family warmed to Blake's right away. Her parents even managed to get over the fact that he wasn't a doctor, lawyer, or millionaire. Apparently, "successful real estate agent" made the approved list as well. Her parents were civil to each other and friendly to everyone else, which was more than she'd hoped for. Now they watched with smiles on their faces and she and Blake made their way to the end of the petaled path.

They kept the ceremony itself very short and sweet, lasting no longer than ten minutes. They vowed to love, comfort, and respect each other – honor, support and cherish one another, in sickness and in health, to laugh and cry together, and forsaking all others, be faithful unto each other as long as they both lived.

They exchanged the wedding rings, his - a manly titanium affair, hers a slim band of rose-gold that cupped perfectly around her engagement ring.

"I pronounce you man and wife!" The minister smiled. "What God has joined together, let no man put asunder. Blake, you may kiss your bride."

He turned to her and grinned, wiggling his eyebrows. Then his hand was securely pressed against her back. *Oh my – he's going to – eek!*

Blake dipped her backwards and kissed her with an energy and love that completely chased away any doubts she might have of his commitment to her. She twined her fingers in his hair and kissed him back. Their first kiss – more wonderful than she could have imagined.

Their little crowd of guests whooped and hollered and whistled. When Blake at last lifted her to her feet once more, the violinist broke into a joyful rendition of "A Thousand Years."

Oh, this love! I never imagined anything like this! Penny walked with her new husband to the corner of the backyard they'd arranged for the 'reception' area, the guests following.

A lace-clothed table laden with sweets greeted them. She'd painted beautiful watercolor signs for the different delicacies, and around the trays of treats were sprigs of greenery and flowers. Instead of a huge cake, Penny had elected for an adorable cupcake tower with a small cake to cut at the top.

Oh! The cake-cutting! If he dares to get frosting all over my face....

Bryce felt like he would burst, watching his younger brother and his new wife cut their cake together. *He's married. Wow.*

The family talked and laughed together and the photographer hovered like a hummingbird, taking pictures left and right. The violinist played softly, the music an undertone for the happy voices.

Cara wiped tears from her eyes and took a bite of a fluffy vanilla cupcake, smiling at Penny.

Then his phone buzzed in the pocked of his gray dress pants. He slipped it out and looked at the screen.

Monty's private number.

He excused himself and walked around the side of the house to answer it, leaning against the bricks. "Monty, what's up?"

"Well – I wish I was calling to say congratulations to your brother and the new Mrs. Reynolds – but something urgent has come up."

Bryce listened as his boss explained what was unfolding. And it was definitely urgent.

Cara silently appeared at his side, one hand clasping the satiny peacock blue skirt of her bridesmaid dress. A question crinkled her forehead.

He nodded. "Understood." He replaced the phone in his pocket. Looked down at his wife. "We need to go."

"We do?" She caught her lip between her pearly teeth. "You know I'm not certified yet." Her agent status was as yet unfinalized – and there was so much more to teach her. But there was no time for that now. They'd been summoned.

"Trust me, after this mission – you will be." *And I need you with me.*

"Well then." Cara lifted her chin, her eyes glinting an obsidian hue instead of gray – determination darkening them. "We'd better say our goodbyes." She spun in place, headed back to the reception.

He stopped her with a hand on her – *woah* – much-stronger-now-arm. Three months of training had taken its effect. "This could get dangerous. Are you ready?"

"I'm ready." Her voice held firm resolve. *She really is ready. And so am I.*

"Let's go."

THE END

The Adventures Continue

MARKDOWN, #3 in the I.C.E. Agency series

Special Agent MARKDOWN and his wife, Agent ANGELWING, are a dynamic force to be reckoned with. But when the day of reckoning comes and their personal secrets from the past are brought to light, will they be able to withstand the trial by fire?

Bryce and Cara Reynolds, AKA Agents ASHBURN and DIAMOND, have worked hard for their places at the top of the Agency's list of best operatives. Can they sacrifice it all when a cry for help comes from the pair to whom they owe so much? And will the cost of true friendship be too high?

The dangers are even greater, old enemies resurface, and the agents will have to use the very last ounce of their resources and brainpower if they want to survive being alienated from the Agency and forced to plunge into the depths of the underworld in Cairo, Moscow, and London to dredge up the answers and once more save the day.

...Coming Soon!

Acknowledgements

Well, firstly, huge thanks go to the dear people who read my first novel, *ASHBURN*, and told me they loved it – or even better, wrote Amazon reviews! Hint-hint! ;)

Another big thank-you is due to the Grzybowski sisters, Victoria and Sarah Grace, who were some of my beta-readers for this book. Your reactions were priceless!

Mama & Daddy, you're seriously the best. I can't imagine more supportive, loving, encouraging parents than the two of you. The pride you take in my writing (and all my other efforts) makes my heart joyful. I love you both so much! Mama, your edit suggestions helped clear up the details in this story... what would creative big-picture me do without detail-person you? Not much, that's what! :)

Mark & Steven – rock on, brothers. Can't wait to see what your future holds. I'm so proud of you both!

Google, I salute thee. You make me sound like I know what I'm talking about. Google Earth and Wikipedia were also very helpful in the creation and imagination stage of this story. You made deciding the location of Cooper's private island so fun.

And finally, thank you, Lord, for the breath I breathe, the overwhelming blessings, and your everlasting love for me. I am nothing without you. May my writing praise your name and draw others into your presence!

About the Author

Julia Erickson has always adored reading. As a little girl, she even read while rollerblading, floating in the pool, and climbing trees. Her love of words and expressive personality naturally flowed into writing her own stories. Off the pages, Julia is also a budding graphic designer, photographer, and blogger. She loves to sing and dance and has her own handcrafted-jewelry business. Sparkle and style and colors are some of her favorite things! Growing up homeschooled all the way (Thanks, Mom!) allowed her to nurture her many hobbies. She loves her Lord and Savior, and believes the Bible is the best and truest story ever told.

Connect with her here:

On Facebook!

http://Facebook.com/JuliaErickson

On her Blog, Julia's Journal:

http://jewelsbyjulia-lauren.blogspot.com

www.ingramcontent.com/pod-product-compliance
Lightning Source LLC
Chambersburg PA
CBHW07084525062 6
47159CB00003B/944